THE FROST FAIR AFFAIR

TANSY RAYNER ROBERTS

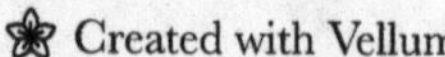 Created with Vellum

For Nancy Blackett
whom, I am quite sure,
became a spy

and Susan Walker
who kept everyone fed

CONTENTS

DRAMATIS PERSONAE

Miss Mnemosyne "Mneme" Seabourne, a notorious
young lady

Juno Jupiter, the Duchess of Storm, recently married
and equally notorious

Henry Jupiter, the Duke of Storm, a happily married
member of the Court of Lords, with a splendid
townhouse

Mr Charles Thornbury, a spellcracker of note

Mr Galbreath Sevinny, an anti-royalist Parliamentarian

Mrs Ceto Sevinny, a fashionable wife of an anti-royalist
Parliamentarian

Mrs Fenchurch, a printer's wife with many small
children

Mr Fenchurch, a printer

Lady Liesl of Sandwich, an eligible young lady

The Countess of Balmady, an influential lady of a
certain age

Mrs Threnod, the companion of an influential lady of a
certain age

Luce, a cider-wife

Elsie, a cider-wife's wife

Bellings, a butler

Nanny Sauvignon, a barely-there chaperone

Thomas, a coachman turned sleigh driver

Hermes Fiero, a celebrity

Figgy, a seat-filler

Lars Zephyr, an inventive tutor

Queen Aud of the Teacup Isles, a monarch

Mr Octavian Swift, a consultant

Mrs Marchwairing, a housekeeper

An unnamed glass-blower

Mr Seabourne, an enthusiastic scholar, less enthusiastic
husband and supportive papa. Barely appears in this
story.

Mrs Galatea Seabourne, a matchmaking mamma, mistress of Shellwich Standing. Far too busy to appear in this story

Miss Metis Seabourne, a pragmatic cousin who cleverly avoids appearing in this story

Basil, a glass hedgehog

NOBLEWOMEN & NOTORIETY

It was a very peculiar thing, to be notorious.

Miss Mnemosyne Seabourne had always been one for avoiding public attention. As the wealthy, unfettered daughter of a legendary family, the last thing she wanted was to capture attention as 'one of those Seabournes.' Since she first came of age, her goal in life was to avoid the state of marriage until she could find that rarest of creatures: a husband she could tolerate. The best way to do this was to ensure one was forgotten about as often as possible.

Mneme's method was to cultivate a reputation of dullness and mediocrity. When she absolutely *had to* attend a ball or public assembly, she dedicated herself to being the least appealing wallflower of the company. Her wit and sparkle were kept for private circles, and trusted friends.

It worked for a long time. Her greatest success was the endless frustration of her mamma, who could not understand how a respectable daughter with a reasonable dowry was such a failure at catching husbands.

But all that was before… before the matter of the elopement and the rescue of the Duke of Storm. Before

Mneme's world was turned upside down by a family scandal. Before Last Season.

(Before a certain spellcracker with rolled-up shirt sleeves caught her attention and made her think that, perhaps, she had found a man worthy of marriage.)

Notoriety was the first consequence Mneme suffered from Last Season's scandal, thanks largely to the discreet arrest and rather less discreet criminal trial of a Certain Female Relative of the Seabourne family. The Tower of Thyme was where the Queen always banished high-ranking magical criminals. It was not a discreet punishment. Society quickly flooded with rumours about how such a matter could possibly have come about.

Mneme faced whispers and pointing fingers everywhere she went. Some admired her for her role in the Duke's rescue — especially those who were friends with the other ladies involved. Others spread far nastier rumours, or gossiped meanly about her marriage prospects.

One thing was for sure, everyone knew who she was. All that work of becoming a non-entity was now wasted. Mneme received three offers of marriage in the first week after the trial (two patronising, one downright insulting), and it was quite a task to refuse all three suitors gracefully while hiding their proposals from her family.

Cousin Metis made the rather sensible decision to set sail for the Continent on a Grand Tour immediately. Mneme sometimes thought wistfully that she should have taken up her cousin's offer to join her for a twelve-month at least, until the worst of it died down.

But she could not. She had work to do. A mission, for the first time in her life.

Instead of running away from it all, Mneme chose to winter in Town: her least favourite of all the Teacup Isles. She would hurl herself directly into the lion's den of invitations, social engagements and urban entertainments, a world where gossip was a currency higher placed than silver or silk. Far from her beloved home and garden and solitude.

It would all be worth it. It had to be worth it. If she was to be notorious, then she would use that notoriety for something constructive. She had work to do, and Town was the only place where she could realise her vision.

Accommodation, at least, was not an issue. Mneme's new bosom friend and cousin-by-marriage, the Duchess of Storm, insisted that Mneme join her at the ducal residence. Storm Bolt, one of many properties owned by Mneme's cousin Henry, was a grand city manor featuring four secret passages, twelve maids, and three libraries.

Mneme was grateful for the offer, and for Juno's friendship. Living in Town was a strain on her usual sensibilities, but the sheer magnitude and breadth of those three ducal libraries helped a lot. Also from here, she would be able to continue her pleasurable acquaintance with Mr Charles Thornbury, the Duke's personal spellcracker, who was obliged to be in Town supporting his employer while the Court of Lords was in session.

(Mr Thornbury and Mneme were not technically engaged to be married, though their understanding was such that an engagement might be forthcoming in the future, once all the fuss had settled down, and Mneme could bear to let him anywhere near her parents.)

Had she remained at home on the Isle of Memory all winter, at her modest family estate, Mneme might have hoped for a few visits from her suitor. After all, Mr Thornbury had the convenience of portal travel at his fingertips, as did all gentlemen of means. Ladies were forbidden to travel by portal, which meant that Mneme would have been reduced to pining and sighing, awaiting Mr Thornbury's visits without ever being able to initiate her own.

Also, visits would have been supervised by her mamma, a trying experience for all concerned.

For convenience of courtship as well as her campaign, Storm Bolt was the best possible choice. Though of course, the campaign was the priority. Completely. Entirely.

Mneme was aflame with passion for her new cause, and for that she would put up with any number of stares and whispers and social gatherings. It was such a terrible injustice that the gentlemen of the Teacup Isles were able to pop about via portal whenever they chose, while social convention forbade women from doing the same.

The tyranny of distance enforced upon her sex had long been taken for granted as the way of things: a bitter inconvenience that must be endured, like childbirth or corsetry. But they lived in an age where corsetry had fallen out of fashion, and amulets could be purchased to regulate or even prevent the conception of children. Why should women still be forced to travel from island to island in such dreadfully old fashioned and tiresome vehicles as swan-shaped boats, or lace-draped carriages?

During the incident Last Season, about which the least said the better, Mneme had found herself faced with a choice: to step through a portal and rescue her cousin Henry from an unfortunate marriage, or hang back and let Mr Thornbury attempt a rescue unaided. She chose adventure, and never felt the slightest regret about it. She was joined by a bevy of equally brave unmarried ladies, who risked their reputations to save the day, and the Duke. While they all faced heightened notoriety thanks to their association with the Duke's abduction, not a whisper had spread about their unladylike mode of transportation in the middle of it all.

That, at least, they had been spared. And yet… Mneme could not help but be annoyed about the whole affair.

The heavens had not fallen in upon them. No thunderbolt incinerated them for their boldness. The only consequence suffered by Mneme and her friends after breaking one of society's greatest restrictions upon women was that they arrived where they needed to be, quickly and at great convenience.

It had to stop. Mneme was going to change the world, for ladies like herself.

Notorious, or not.

"MUST WE WALK EVERY DAY?" Mneme asked Juno, as the two of them perambulated around the shady avenue between the Museum of Antiquities and the Library of Arcane Promises.

She did not mind the exertion, but she did rather mind the faces darting out at her from behind fur hoods and parasols, checking to see if it really was one of those scandalous Seabourne girls, arm-in-arm with the new and equally controversial Duchess of Storm. Mouths formed whispers, not quite loud enough to be heard across the chilly street, but clear in their meaning.

"Is that —"

"It must be!"

"Daughter of —"

"Niece of —

"Cousin of —"

"And that with her, the new —"

"Married to —"

"You heard about that wedding, I suppose?"

"Oh, you haven't heard? Let me tell you."

"La!"

"Teacups and hedgehogs."

Honestly, the way they all carried on, you'd think she

was the Silver Spoon Strangler, not a perfectly ordinary young lady who happened to have an embarrassing aunt.

"It is important to be seen," said Juno proudly, her head thrown back. Garbed in the most extraordinary hooded confection of a walking coat, recently shipped in from the Continent, she was in her element. Notoriety suited her, especially now it came matched with a title.

'Duchess' went with everything.

At the end of the shady avenue, as they approached the Arcade of Ladylike Dainties, the two of them turned with a graceful and practiced spin, heading back the way they came. Juno always insisted on several laps of the avenue before she allowed them inside the arcade for tea, chocolate and browsing.

Mneme appreciated the nudge, really, though she did feel that the daily promenade in icy winds was excessive. "I'm certain we could be seen somewhere warm and indoors."

"Don't fuss so," said Juno. "How do you expect to achieve greatness if no one knows who you are?"

"They all know who I am," Mneme reminded her.

"They *think* they know, but seeing is different to gossiping. Seeing you in a fine coat, walking about like you have nothing to hide will do far more for your campaign than printing leaflets, and muttering in corners with bluestockings."

"I need to do more than show off this year's winter fashion," Mneme protested. Still, she could not hold back the inner glow that took hold with Juno's words. *Achieve greatness.* Yes, indeed. That was exactly what she wished to do. "I want them to listen to what I have to say."

"The Court of Lords is in session for thirty-six more days," said Juno, who had clearly been thinking about it. "And that overlaps with the Parliament of Gentles, which opens shortly. If the dreaded portal issue was actually against the law, it would be straightforward enough — you need only arrange for one Lord to draft a bill to allow portal travel for ladies, and eight more to support it, then arrange for a majority of Parliament to pass it into law."

"Oh, is that all?" said Mneme, indulging in a little sarcasm. "Portal travel is *not* against the law."

"Exactly," said Juno. "That's what makes it all so devilish tricky. If we show our hand before we achieve the tipping point of popularity, some chump will see a chance to pop in and make the ban official."

"I don't see why we need to involve gentlemen at all," said Mneme. "Surely if we attach some significant patronesses to the campaign, and raise awareness with more meetings, perhaps some fundraising…"

"This isn't a charity, nor an opera fund," said Juno. "You want to change the minds of the great and good as to what is respectable. If ladies are the only ones discussing it, then it will never be seen as a significant issue. No, we must convince some gentleman to rally to our side, and to raise the topic where the public gallery will hear it. Not my husband, of course," she added firmly.

"But Henry agrees —"

"What use is him agreeing with us? He might be high up in the Lordly food chain on a technicality, but no one takes him seriously at all. What you need is someone respected and conservative to believe this is all his own idea and pipe up about it in public. Then you need some unpopular rabble-rouser of a parliamentarian, like that Sevinny fellow who holds such sway with the anti-royalist party, to shout it down, also in public. If we get the timing right, the crusty old Lords will all decide that portal travel is the sort of thing their grandmothers would have approved of, and that's how you change the world." She snapped her fingers elegantly.

Mneme felt quite dizzy. It was a wonder that Juno was

not out of breath. "I was rather hoping we could convince the Queen to take our side," she admitted. "If we could get near her to ask…"

Juno scoffed. "You expect a female monarch to take an interest in the rights of women? She has all the rights she could ever need, and hardly travels beyond Town and Court. Her currency is popularity, not justice. Not to mention, half of the Court of Lords — the half who snooze through lunch, mostly — are still so traumatised at having a young female ruler in the first place, they'll complain from here to eternity if they think she approves of a thing. She's been trying to fund schools for orphans for the last three years, and they obstruct her at every turn."

"That's all most discouraging," said Mneme in dismay.

"Ah, well, that's without factoring in our secret weapon."

That was alarming, not least because of her friend's tone of voice suggested she was planning something exceedingly scandalous (or, at least, rather naughty). "Juno, what on earth do you have in mind?" Mneme demanded.

The new Duchess of Storm laughed long and loud, in a way that lesser-ranked ladies would never be allowed. She had embraced her new status with a confident ease of which few ladies under thirty years were capable. "Oh, your face. My dear Mneme. What on earth must you be imagining?"

It was not so long ago that Mneme knew — not suspected, but *knew* — that Juno was the kind of person who was ruthless and ambitious enough to use magical means to catch a Duke for a husband. It might not be nice to question the ethics of the lady who had been such a good friend to her… but it was also not unreasonable.

Mneme was notorious now. Why limit herself to what was considered nice? "Forgive me if I blanch at the use of the word 'weapon' after what transpired with my family," she said, rather sharply.

"It was a metaphor, you goose." Juno pulled her fur hood around her face as a particularly chill breeze swept up the avenue to pinken their cheeks. "I was speaking of the Senate. They should take our side with a little persuasion, and I believe *they* will be the allies we need for a successful campaign."

Mneme blinked several times, the chill wind making her eyes prickle. Her family were hardly political, but she knew the basics of how governance worked in the Teacup Isles. The Queen ruled overall, but all laws, governance and financial decisions ran through the paired bodies of the Court of Lords and the Parliament of Gentles. That was the way of things. "What Senate?" she asked, feeling foolish.

Juno squeezed her arm in a convivial manner. "The secret one, of course! The only way that women get anything done around here. Are you famished? I'm famished. Let's go in for tea."

SNOW AND THE SECRET SENATE

The first proper snow of winter fell later that day.
It dabbed and floated in gentle spirals through
the grey streets of the Isle of Town, gathering weight and
speed.

Mnemosyne watched it from the window seat of the
second library of Storm Bolt, the ducal residence. This was
her favourite of the libraries, the smallest and least showy
of the three, and the one where she could most easily
evade other people for hours at a time. She had adopted
this particular library seat as a child, on the rare occasions
when the various branches of the Seabourne family came
together in Town rather than one of the country estates.

It was the furthest away from anything else in the
house. Even the maids only dusted in here once a week, as
Henry's Great Grandmamma Jupiter had once declared
that too much cleanliness was bad for the longevity of
paper. Mneme suspected that, much like herself, Henry's
Great Grandmamma Jupiter preferred books to people.

She was still chewing over the information that Juno
had revealed to her earlier that day, over tea and crumpets
in the Arcade of Ladylike Dainties.

A Secret Senate! Otherwise known, according to Juno's sources, as the Great Discretion. While it was not an official governing body, the group was made up of the wives, mothers and occasionally sisters and daughters of past and present members of the Court of Lords and the Parliament of Gentles. Clearly a hub of great power and efficacy.

By all accounts, it was the Great Discretion who quietly ensured that corsetry fell out of fashion, and contraception amulets fell in… both stunning social changes that offered new freedoms to Mneme's generation.

This raised an important question: if there was indeed a Secret Senate of Ladies, using their matrimonial and womanly wiles to enact vital change on behalf of women in society, then why on earth had they allowed the great injustice around portal travel to continue for so long?

The door opened behind Mneme, and she heard the sonorous voice of Bellings, the butler of Storm Bolt. Cousin Henry was a wild, aimless puppy dog of a man with no more sense than the gods gave a dormouse, and yet he had marvellous luck in hiring staff. Bellings was one of a team of excellent butlers who staffed the various ducal residences; he was so good at his job that Mneme could not even resent the fact that he, more than anyone else in this household, always knew exactly where she was at any given time.

"Mr Charles Thornbury," Bellings now boomed into the library before disappearing back behind the door in a haze of competence. "Personal Spellcracker to his Grace, the Duke of Storm!"

There he was. Her Thornbury. Rather dishevelled, one of his coat sleeves looking quite askew. "No need to announce me," he called behind him with a weary impatience. "I live and work here. Still!"

No response, from the best butler this side of the river.

Mneme allowed a warm smile to cross her face. Possibly she did not even have a choice in the matter. "Hello, there."

Thornbury's own face warmed up rather quickly as he took her in. "Hello, there."

They gazed soppily at each other for a moment or two, which was just enough time for Nanny Sauvignon, Henry's old nurse, to slide into the library with a basket full of knitting and a cheeky twinkle. "Don't mind me, dears," she said sweetly, and settled into a corner of the room with her back turned to them.

There was that butler competence again, supplying all the needs of the household before they even thought of them — including appropriately discreet chaperonage for a nearly-engaged couple, living under the ducal roof.

Mneme usually hired her own chaperone: Mrs Paula Daze, a lady novelist of her acquaintance. But Mrs Daze disliked Town as much as Mneme did. Besides, the whole benefit of having married female friends of one's acquaintance was that one could mostly do away with the whole chaperone issue.

Mostly.

Darting a sheepish look in the direction of the nurse, Thornbury crossed the library and sat beside Mneme on the window seat. He kissed her gently on the cheek, careful not to smack his lips too loudly (the old woman had ears like a bat, and gossiped with *everyone*) then took both her hands in his, which were not as cold as you might expect for a man just returned to the house.

"You didn't walk home, then," Mneme said archly. "Portal?"

"Portal," he confirmed. "His Grace has had me popping in and out of drawing rooms all afternoon, delivering invitations for this soiree he's hosting for the Duchess next week."

"That's not your usual line of work, is it?" Thornbury's tasks for the Duke were generally magical in nature — such as ensuring that Henry did not fall prey to any charms or hexes. This threat had lessened somewhat once Henry chose a wife.

"Flying paper doves," Thornbury said with a wince. "My job was to ensure they got to their targets without falling into fireplaces, or being shot down by the magical defences of each household."

"Should have made paper pigeons, instead," said Mneme, who was a dab hand at invitational magic. "They fly faster and don't take any nonsense. It is sweet, though," she added. "Henry wants to make a fuss of Juno's name day, since they didn't have an especially grand wedding."

"Oh," said Thornbury, pretending to be serious. "Is that your way of saying you want a full seven-night gala when your name day comes around?"

Mneme's eyes widened. "No, thank *you*. Books, chocolate and solitude are my three favourite gifts."

"I'll make sure to wrap you a bouquet of absent friends and relatives when the big day comes around."

Mneme liked this very much, the simple domesticity of a quiet conversation at the end of the day. If not for the presence of Nanny S. in the corner, it might be a preview of the life they were to have together, when matters were sorted out to a satisfactory conclusion. "You didn't get to work on your lecture at all, then?"

"Not today. I'll have a stab at it later tonight. How was your morning? More scheming and cakes with the Duchess?"

"Plotting, thank you," Mneme said primly. "It sounds so much more official than scheming."

Thornbury darted a quick glance at the nurse and then shifted closer. His bare hand brushed the back of Mneme's wrist, making her shiver. "Plotting," he corrected himself gravely. "Any progress?"

She gave him a stern look. "A little more now that I know there is such a thing as a Secret Senate!"

"I'm sure I don't know what you're talking about."

"Don't pretend!"

"If I did know, I shouldn't. Secret ladies business. Nothing to do with me."

"Juno thinks they'll be a big help to the campaign."

"Really," said Thornbury with a slight frown.

"You don't think so?"

"I didn't say that."

Mneme raised both eyebrows. "But you don't think so."

"I think that the rich and powerful can't always be relied upon to do the logical thing in anyone's best interest," said Thornbury, looking more serious than ever. "If the Great Discretion are half as powerful and effective as rumour suggests, then why would they let something like the portal restriction continue for so long? Don't take their support for granted. You'll have to win them over."

This was exactly what Mneme had been thinking, but it was so much more real and depressing coming from his mouth.

He noticed, of course. The trouble with being courted by a spellcracker was that his job relied on him being highly observant. "Don't be discouraged," Thornbury said now, kissing her gently just above her eyebrow. "I have great faith in your abilities. Look what you achieved with a table of teacups Last Season. But… don't rely solely on Juno's advice when it comes to the titled upper crust. She has barely been a Duchess for five minutes. Is Lady Liesl in Town? She might even have a membership to you-know-what. If not her, then her aunts and grandmother."

"She's *supposed* to be coming to Town this winter,"

Mneme said glumly. "But last I heard she had only just set out by boat from the Isle of Sandwich, and that's at least a week's travel. If this cold snap settles, she might suffer further delays."

Which was of course the point of her portal campaign. Why should ladies drudge their way through snow, sleet, swan-shaped boats and ill-smelling carriages when there was magic in the world?

FIND US AT THE FROST FAIR

*T*he cold snap settled. By the next day, snow was a thick layer everywhere. Horse-drawn cabs were retired in favour of the occasional horse-drawn sledge on the icy roads. Salt was strewn liberally around to help with walking from block to block. Of course, those gentlemen privileged enough to have portal access were not hampered in the slightest in their visits to the Court or their clubs, though a few might be mildly inconvenienced by the slowing of supplies and deliveries.

Mnemosyne thought of her friend Lady Liesl, still in transit between the Isles of Sandwich and Town. It made her shiver to think of it.

Juno only allowed one day of housebound solitude before she rebelled, knocking on Mneme's bedroom door almost as soon as the tray of tea and toast arrived. "Get up, lazybones," she hollered, swooping into Mneme's room wearing a brand-new pelisse the shade of a fresh mulberry. "We're going on an adventure."

"I don't care what you say," said Mneme, who had been perfectly comfortable with her breakfast and a book in bed, thank you very much. "I won't engage in snowball fights, nor street croquet. My sporting prowess is for warm weather only."

"But darling," said Juno, tugging at the curtains with a complete ineptitude that was somehow reassuring. "The printer said three days, didn't he? Your pamphlets should be ready!"

That was enough to have Mneme sitting up straight and pushing off the covers. "It's eight blocks away!"

"Do you think I've been building up your walking skills for nothing? Best boots forward, Miss Seabourne!"

THE WALK to Fenchurch and Sons: Master Printers was not as terrifying as Mneme imagined — she and Juno both had warming charms on their gloves and socks, which went a long way to mitigating the wintry chill of the day.

There was a surprising number of people out and about, despite the lack of traffic on the streets. Occasional children slid by, pulled by obliging adults on small sledges that had been dusted out of attics for the occasion.

Still, Mneme was rather longing for a hot cup of tea by the time they arrived at Brill Street. She found herself glancing around in hope of a chocolate shop, rather than paying attention to where she was going.

It was Juno who spotted the sign first. "Dash it, they're closed!" she announced. Clearly, being married to Henry was having an effect on her vocabulary.

"What?" said Mneme, hurrying forward. The door was indeed locked fast, and there was a card in the window that read: *Relocated due to weather. Find us at the Frost Fair.* "Is there really a Frost Fair this year?"

"Goodness," said Juno with glee. "The Scamander's frozen over then, what fun! We'll have to head home and change. Can't wear any old thing to a Frost Fair. There hasn't been one for years. The forecast must be for snow and more snow."

"Must be," said Mneme, shivering despite her warming charms. "I understand food sellers and the like taking their wares to the ice. But a printer?"

"Printers most of all," said a male voice, very near them. Both women jumped; they had not seen him approach. He was a small gentleman, with a shock of dark hair sticking out from beneath his hat, and a carelessly-tied cravat that clashed badly with his coat. Mneme didn't know him at all, but he clearly recognised Juno, as he nodded his head to her. "Your Grace. Pardon the interruption."

"Not at all," said Juno, looking wildly intrigued. "Are you here for the print-works also, Mr Sevinny?"

"I was." He raised himself on the toes of his boots to peer in the window, looking most disgruntled. "I had an order for several copies of a satirical print by a friend of mine. I suppose I must try to find this printing fellow on the ice and hope that he brought the pages with him along with his press, instead of leaving them locked up in the shop."

"Wouldn't it be foolish to move something as heavy as a printing press on to the ice?" said Mneme. What if it breaks?"

"That's the risk, of course," said the gentleman with a shrug. "But if it's anything like last Frost Fair, the river's already covered with braziers, sledges and half a tonne of people walking to and fro. They'll have stamped it down it good and hard to test the strength before taking anything valuable out there. You'd be amazed what fellows are prepared to risk to make their fortune selling sixpenny souvenir cards. It's all about proving you were there, of course, and the cards wouldn't sell half so well if they weren't printed on the spot."

"There was a Frost Fair the first year I was Out," said Juno, sounding charmed. "Chestnuts, hot cider and a terribly talented tightrope walker who crossed the Scamander from shore to shore on a single wire."

The gentleman's eyes lit up. "Was that the fair with the elephant?"

"Goodness, no. I'm not that old!" She fluttered her eyelashes at him a little. "I was promised I'd see an elephant, but alas. Not that year."

"Maybe this winter will bring you better fortune." The gentleman drew back, and bowed to them both. A short, abrupt motion — far shallower than you might expect anyone to bend in the presence of a known Duchess. "Ladies."

"Goodness," Juno murmured as he walked away. "What wouldn't I give to see what he's printing."

"Do you know that gentleman?" Mneme asked.

"Only by repute. He's at least as notorious as you are, my dear, by profession rather than family scandal. That is Galbreath Sevinny, the anti-royalist."

"Oh," said Mneme. "In that case we were honoured to get even half a bow out of him. Isn't he that fellow you were hoping would denounce our campaign, so the stuffiest Earls and Lords would support it?"

"Mmm," Juno agreed. "I may have been wrong about that. I don't think that young man can be predicted to do anything one expects." She shook herself out of a moment of reverie. "Come along. The Frost Fair! Your pamphlets. And, if we're very lucky, an elephant."

GETTING to the Frost Fair was more of a production than expected, not only because both ladies were so fatigued and cold after their long walk back to Storm Bolt, they required several rounds of tea and sandwiches to regain their strength. By then, Henry had returned home with several gentlemen friends, who were so delighted at interrupting the luncheon (a casual meal generally reserved for ladies) that more ham and fruit and cheese was called for until it became an entire civilised party.

There was no sign of Mr Thornbury. When pressed, Henry claimed to have no idea where one might find his personal spellcracker. ("Probably drifted into a library and got distracted, eh, what!") By the time they set out for the Frost Fair, they were a crowd of eight including a Marquess, a famous poet, two uniformed members of the Queen's Guard, and a political secretary who was following the Duke around in order to get him to sign off on a stack of paperwork for the Court of Lords, and had so far been fed in three separate households while engaged in this task.

"For goodness' sake, sign the dratted things before we set off, Henry, or there will be contracts papering the river," complained Juno, but what with one thing and another, the secretary was still attached to their party when they left Storm Bolt.

Also with them: four of Henry's favourite hounds. Juno had put her foot down when they came south for the winter, insisting that he not bring every animal he owned into their splendid town house. Four was their compromise. Each of the hounds, like Henry himself, were large and sprawling creatures who liked to try to run in several directions at once despite the leashes that dangled at their necks.

The wide ribbon river of Scamander ran in a spiralling circle, creating a smaller island in the centre of the Isle of Town. The central island, known to all as Court, contained Wistworia Palace, the Court and Parliament buildings, several fine parks, an opera house and a temple. Mneme had visited the Isle of Court a few times in her youth, and associated it with a feeling of constant anxiety that she might break something precious.

The freezing over of the river meant, of course, that the ferries and swan-shaped boats that usually made up for an inadequacy of bridges were grounded. The more entrepreneurial ferrymen had either winched wheels on to their boats in order to continue earning their daily coin, or else hired sledges to tow about by hand, or horse.

The secret to a Frost Fair was that nothing was planned in advance. You never knew until it happened whether the river would freeze over in a given winter, and if so, if it would turn out to be a long enough cold snap to stay frozen.

Mneme's mamma had always spoken airily of frost magic, assuring young Mneme that such things were in the hands of the Queen and her magisters. But now, stepping on to the frozen river, Mneme felt no presence of magic within the ice.

Upon it, certainly. There was small magic everywhere: in the braziers that burned hot without falling straight through into the river; in the warming charms that kept the affluent from feeling the chill too badly; and of course in the displays and exhibitions.

There were dancers, artisans, conjurers, buskers, charmsmiths and brothel-keepers, all rubbing shoulders and jostling for space. The tents, stalls and temporary dwellings that had sprung up overnight fell into a sort of mess of streets and alleys with no logic to it. An orange seller hawked her wares next to an apothecary, next to a teller of fortunes.

The air was rich with the scents of perfume, cinnamon and roasting meat; the crowd was alive with the thrill of something illicit and edged with danger.

"Look out for printers," Juno commanded her small troop of followers, including her husband.

"Those robbers," snorted one of the guards, a youngster who had clearly joined up for the uniform. "I hear they charge five pennies for one of those cards. Just because it's signed to say *printed upon the ice*. I bet they fake it."

"Sixpence," said the other, tilting his hat so as to show off his plumes to greater effect. "They can't fake it, not if they print the date. No one knew we'd have a frost fair this week. Cheaper for them to be authentic, don't you know?"

"I shall have a toffee apple," announced Henry, and was promptly distracted by a Punch and Judy show. The portable puppet theatre, brightly striped in scarlet and white, was squashed between a sausage stall and a silversmith. A carpet (already damp and rather pungent) lay in front of the theatre, for the audience to sit upon.

This was not a show for children, though a few managed to duck away from their parents long enough to catch a scene or two of the bawdy jokes and brutal antics.

"I hate those puppets," sighed Juno, even as every man in their party was instantly captivated, guffawing at the comedy violence of Mr Punch and the policeman. "I'd like to see Judy take that stick and give Punch a taste of his own medicine."

She plucked impatiently at Mneme's sleeve. "Come on. Let's leave these gadabouts to their entertainment. I think I see our printer over there."

In the end, they tried four different printer's stalls before they located Fenchurch and Sons, just past the Tethys Bridge. The printing press was housed inside a shabby-looking tent papered with posters and flyers, between a glass-blower's stand and a cider tent. A roaring crowd were already queueing to purchase those infamous sixpenny cards signed and dated to prove they had been printed right here, today, on the frozen Scamander.

The printer's tent, and its sales table out front, was staffed by a harried-looking pregnant woman with two toddlers at her heels, and an older boy who gravely took the pennies and handed over the cards. The curtains were pinned back wide so all customers could see the magnificent printing press was genuinely here, grinding away to stamp more cards.

"Is Mr Fenchurch around?" Juno asked when she and Mneme finally reached the front of the queue.

The woman gave her a filthy look. "If he was, don't you think he'd be working same as me? What are you after, madam?"

Mneme nudged her way in, smiling politely. "I'm Miss Seabourne. I had a stack of pamphlets to collect? The shop is closed."

"Collected already," the woman said shortly. "Next!"

"Wait. Collected by whom?" Mneme asked, rather in shock.

"Your maid, I suppose."

"I don't have a maid."

The busy woman gave her a glare that could have thawed the Frost Fair from edge to edge. "Is that my problem? She signed for it."

"Show us," Juno demanded, in the voice of a woman who was about to make a scene.

The printer's wife sighed, reached under the table, and slapped a ledger before them. She motioned the next customer forward. Shunted to one side, Mneme flipped the book to the last page and saw an indecipherable scrawl just below the neater signature of Mr G. Sevinny, who had collected a box of Prints: Satirical.

"This could be anyone!" she protested. "You just — let my pamphlets walk off in the hands of a stranger?"

Mrs Fenchurch shrugged again, though she was looking rather embarrassed now, like she was rather ashamed of herself. "Well, how was I to know?" she said weakly. "Who'd want a bunch of pamphlets about transport politics? You'll have to wait if you want them doing over. This ice might only last a few days, and the profit from a Frost Fair means new shoe leather for all my kids."

Who'd want a bunch of pamphlets about transport politics? Yes, indeed. That was the question.

Juno leaned in, reading over Mneme's shoulder. "Not sure what's worse," she said thoughtfully. "If they were stolen by some stranger… or by someone who knows exactly who you are."

"Do you recognise that signature?" Mneme asked, wondering from where that particular thought had come.

But Juno, quite uncharacteristically, refused to say more.

DISCRETION BEST SERVED COLD

The Frost Fair was all very entertaining, but getting properly warm afterwards took more than a couple of cozy charms. Even with soup and a steaming cup of chocolate for supper, Mneme felt the need to retire to her room with the fireplace blazing, and a quilted bed jacket wrapped over her nightgown.

Annoyed but clearly in the wrong, Mrs Fenchurch had agreed to replace the pamphlets within two or three days, when she had time between runs of souvenir cards.

It was more than frustrating. Even more frustrating was Juno's refusal to tell Mneme why she was so disturbed by that signature in the ledger.

Still, this was a minor setback. The last thing Mneme wanted was to rush the delicate business of enacting social change.

Tomorrow, she had an invitation to supper with the Countess of Balmady's Book Club which, according to Juno, was her best route to the Secret Senate, or the Great Discretion.

~

THE COUNTESS OF BALMADY, as one of the Queen's ladies-in-waiting, resided on the Court side of the River Scamander, which meant traversing the Frost Fair once again.

Juno had arranged for a horse-drawn sleigh, which came with fur wrappings and hot cups of spiced cider as they were dragged across the river.

It was one of the more civilised forms of travel that Mneme had ever experienced, though it could only be achieved on a Duchess's budget.

"I can't believe you didn't read the book," she teased Juno, as they slid along the ice surrounded by the bright lanterns and glittering entertainments of the Frost Fair at night. "It's a book club."

Juno shrugged. "It's one of those books about castles. They're all the same. A governess, a ghost, far more secret passages than is reasonably credible, a long-lost family secret and a murder that everyone has forgotten to solve by the end."

"You still have to read it!" Mneme was faintly outraged by Juno's cavalier attitude.

"Do I, though?" Juno, as ever, was amused by Mneme taking anything seriously.

As they divested themselves of their ungainly layers of wool and fur in the foyer of the Countess' apartment (which, at three floors high, was larger than some town-houses), a familiar figure came towards them: Lady Liesl of Sandwich, wearing sparkling snowflake earrings and a bold celestial blue robe trimmed with white satin, topped off by a crown turban.

"I thought you were travelling," said Mneme as they embraced.

"If anyone asks, we were lucky with the crosswinds," said Liesl, looking innocent. "No bribes were paid to portal watchmen in the least."

"Why, you've turned into quite the rebel," said Juno. "I'm impressed."

"Who has time to travel by sea when there are social niceties to overturn and husbands to catch?" said Liesl with a sniff. "Oh, look, how sweet. Mneme brought a copy of the book."

"It's a book club," said Mneme. "Don't tell me you didn't read it either."

"It's a novel set in some exotic corner of the Continent by some girl our age who has only ever read books about the Continent," said Liesl dismissively. "And there's a ghost in it, probably." She tucked her arm in both of theirs. "Never mind the book, you'll never guess who's here. It's quite the scandal."

By the time they reached the receiving parlour, up a spiral staircase, Liesl and Juno were deeply immersed in their gossip exchange. The two of them had forged a close friendship since Juno beat Liesl to Cousin Henry.

In the Teacup Isles, ballads had been written for far less than the catching of an eligible Duke in matrimony, out from under the nose of a higher-ranked lady of the gentry.

Mneme was not offended to be left out of their chatter. She extricated herself from Liesl's elbow at the first opportunity. Juno's friendship was like a warm blanket that wrapped itself in layers around your head in the middle of the night. It was refreshing to breathe for a moment, without the need for constant conversation.

The parlour was full of ladies and fine magic. Wall sconces lit up the room like burning candles that never ran out of wick or wax. Shimmers of charmwork appeared like shadows, here and there amongst the pretty frocks and elegant decor. Even these, the wealthiest and highest-ranked ladies of Town, all used minor illusions to cover up small flaws, or to make their natural beauty shine that little bit brighter.

Their hostess had provided magic displays for entertainment, also: a shelf of dancing mice near the window, wearing hats that made them look like midwinter gnomes. There was a portrait of an ancestor over the main fireplace, who bowed to every lady that passed by, and occasionally recited a verse of poetry.

Liesl was not the only one wearing snowflake earrings. The Frost Fair had taken fire among the ladies of Town and Court, with winter-themed fashion very much the order of the day. Everything was blue and silver and crystalline, trimmed in white fur or satin or ruffled gauze. One young matron showed off a blown-glass locket that had been *made on the ice*, and another cooed over a hair-brooch featuring a horse-drawn sleigh.

Mneme accepted a cup of tea, embracing her old wallflower identity as the conversation and power games unrolled before her. She had always felt like an outsider at these gatherings of urban nobility, even as a daughter of the esteemed Seabourne family, the niece to a Duchess and (more recently) the cousin to a Duke.

This particular crowd featured many ladies of influence. Mneme had not seen so many wives of the Court of Lords since the 'sewing circles' hosted by her aunt, the former Duchess of Storm, in the years before her death.

(Mneme recalled a parade of important older ladies arriving at Storm Bolt with beautiful sewing baskets that no one ever seemed to open.)

It occurred to her only now that if there was a Secret Senate of ladies, then her mother and aunts must have been card-carrying members… at least until the disgrace of Last Season. And that explained the looks and whispers that had been thrown her way recently, over porcelain cups and plates of Angelica sponge.

Embrace notoriety, she reminded herself, though her natural instinct was to flee to a corner with her book. *At least it means they know who you are. It will be useful to your mission.*

"There you are!" Juno flung herself at Mneme, carrying a plate with three kinds of tiny sandwich upon it. "I must introduce you to our hostess."

~

"So much red hair," murmured the Countess of Balmady in a tone which might have conveyed either envy, or disapproval.

Either way, there wasn't much Mneme could do about it. Red-gold hair and determined chins ran in her family.

"Clearly a Seabourne," agreed the Countess's companion, who was introduced as Mrs Threnod.

Both were ladies 'of a certain age' which was to say, they could have been grandmothers. If they were, you could be sure you would never hear a word about their grandchildren, and they would speak of their sons as if they were feckless youths (even if they were men of forty years or more).

The Countess wore deep navy, her silver hair pinned high, and an old family diamond collar with a snowflake design that must have been made for one of the earliest Frost Fairs, nearly a century ago. Easy enough to follow (or indeed, to lead) fashions that came around every decade or so, when you had a manor full of family jewels. Her companion's outfit was all in shades of grey, far less showy. Mrs Threnod wore an antique lace fichu that not only covered her neckline, but buttoned all the way up her long neck.

"Is your mother well?" asked the Countess, which was honestly a warmer greeting than Mneme had expected, given the frostiness of that lady's expression.

"She is enjoying a winter on the Isle of Bath," said

Mneme, not needing to add the detail that Mamma had retreated to Bath month before winter began, and showed no sign of dislodging herself, to the great dismay of Mr Seabourne.

"That's the spirit," said the Countess, nodding with approval. "Going to ground after family troubles. It's the best way to handle such things."

"Absolutely the best way," agreed Mrs Threnod. The two ladies glared at Mneme, as if expecting her to offer an explanation of why she, too, was not hiding her shame from the world.

Juno, whose Duchess powers were clearly diminished in the face of such antique disdain, was the first to break. "I positively begged my dear Miss Seabourne to winter with me," she burst out. "My husband the Duke is so distracted at this time of year, with the duties of state…"

Mrs Threnod leaned forward, ignoring the Duchess of Storm. "I hear you fancy yourself as something of a writer, Miss Seabourne. *Quite* extraordinary."

"A writer?" said Mneme, confused at this train of conversation. "Why, hardly at all, except…" She froze.

Mrs Threnod pulled a small folded pamphlet from somewhere in her fichu and handed it to the Countess. "Something of a writer," she said, and laughed a croaky wheeze of a laugh. "Or so she thinks."

LATER, as they waited in the foyer for the sleigh to take them home, Mneme was still furious. "Who do those old hags think they are?" she hissed to Juno as they pulled on layers of coats, gloves, over-boots.

"The most powerful ladies of influence in the city?" Juno said pertly.

"Why shouldn't I write a pamphlet? Why shouldn't I

try to make the world better for ladies? Why should I have to grovel for their stamp of approval?" Mneme stared at a window that opened out on to the snowy courtyard beyond the Countess' beautiful apartment. "Why should two ladies like ourselves have to travel at night in the snow, when there must be half a dozen portals in this apartment, all for the convenience of men?"

Juno pulled her fur hood down snugly over her hair. "You're not suggesting we do a Liesl, are you? I don't think there's enough bribes in the world that could cover it up, if we hijacked the Count of Balmady's private portal."

"We shouldn't have to bribe anyone," Mneme muttered. "We are guests."

"Don't take that dried up old lemon-face seriously," Juno assured her. "Your pamphlet was excellent. I read the whole thing, and you know I hardly ever read all the way to the end."

"It was two pages," said Mneme, trying not to smile.

"Exactly. Two whole pages! I was riveted. You have a compelling turn of phrase."

"How did she even get hold of it?" That was what really worried Mneme. "Bad enough that some maid picked up my pamphlets by accident, but how did they get into the hands of the Countess and her Secret Senate so quickly?"

"Oh, darling," said Juno. "Do you really think it was an accident? Look, Thomas is here!"

The two of them scurried out into the freezing air, walking like careful penguins until Juno's chauffeur Thomas was able to boost them comfortably into the hired sleigh.

"Not enough warming charms in the world," Juno sighed, burying her hands in her favourite fur-lined muff. "At least the river won't thaw tonight. But tomorrow, I shall spend every minute in bed with hot chocolate, see if I don't!"

"You think someone stole my pamphlets deliberately?" Mneme said. "And distributed them among the ladies of the Secret Senate? Seems a rather odd choice, to hijack my work and then do it for me."

"There's distribution, and then there's distribution," Juno said darkly as they set off into the night. "You only know of one copy that hit its mark. For all you know, the rest of them are kindling for someone's drawing room fire."

They had to wait a while, halfway across the frozen river, as other traffic was waved through. The Frost Fair was still alive with customers and hucksters on either side of this transit channel, with fires and torches burning merrily with the protective aid of enough spells, Mneme hoped, to keep the heat from sending them all into the chilly drink.

They set off again finally. After a minute or two, Thomas had to yank hard on the reins as a surge of struggling pedestrians crossed in front of their horses' hooves. "Ho there," he called out in warning.

Juno elbowed Mneme. "Why, that's Mrs Fenchurch, isn't it?"

Mneme leaned over and saw the printer's wife, almost doubled over with the weight of the bundles she carried. "Are you all right?"

"You're going back to Brill Street?" asked Juno. "We'll give you a lift."

Mrs Fenchurch made a token protest, but she was clearly exhausted from her day's work, while Juno was still fuelled by her own outrage at the Countess of Balmady. Within moments, Thomas had tucked Mrs Fenchurch into the sleigh with them, and tied her parcels on the back.

"Do have some chocolate, you look done in," said Juno,

with her usual careless generosity. "You aren't carrying that whole printing press home, are you?"

Mrs Fenchurch looked suspicious of the Duchess' largesse, but accepted the cup she was handed. "No, your Grace," she muttered. "Paid the watchmen a shilling to keep an eye on it overnight, after I sent the children home with my sister. Couldn't leave all this stock at the stall, though, it'd get half-inched."

"I suppose that's true," said Juno thoughtfully. "Whereas stealing something as heavy as a printing press would cause enough ruction at least that the watchmen would notice."

"Aye," said Mrs Fenchurch, her cheeks pinkening up a little as she sipped on the chocolate. "No one's getting that iron beast of ours off the river without knocking down half a dozen other tents as they go."

"I'd buy a ticket to that show," said Juno cheerfully. "Thomas, to Brill Street!"

"I can walk once we're on dry land," Mrs Fenchurch said quickly. "It's tricky to get across the river on foot, that's all, with so many folk crossing at once."

"Nonsense," said Juno. "The streets are quite clear enough, and it will barely take us out of our way."

She then set about putting the printer's wife at her ease: a Herculean task, since Mrs Fenchurch had her defences up to maximum.

The suspicion on the face of the printer's wife deepened as Juno rattled on, then began to ease once it became obvious that Juno was none-too-subtly attempting to find out if Mrs Fenchurch remembered anything further about the 'maid' who had 'half-inched' Mneme's pamphlets.

Clearly, it was easier for Mrs Fenchurch to believe they would come to her assistance because they wanted something from her, rather than from the goodness of their hearts.

~

"Flaxen hair, a worsted apron and an eyepatch," said Juno with great satisfaction as she and Mneme finally returned to Storm Bolt, dropping their outer layers as well as their warming charms. "Now all we have to do is find that maid, and the mystery is nearly solved."

"I think she was pulling your leg about the eyepatch," said Mneme.

"Oh yes, but I did enjoy the expression on her face as she came up with it."

"I've been thinking about all this wrong," said Mneme, as they headed up the staircase, grateful to be indoors. "The lack of portal travel is an annoying inconvenience for us. But we have every luxury at our fingertips if we wish: boats and carriages and furs and warming charms. What about the other women in the world? What about the men, even, who can't afford to pay for a public portal?"

"Mneme," said Juno warningly. "This is beginning to sound like it is not a campaign at all, but a revolution."

Mneme said nothing, but her heart rose at the thought of it. Revolution. Wasn't that a better legacy for the Seabourne family than Last Season's terrible scandal? Wasn't it time she did something useful with all the advantages she had been given?

How very freeing it was to be notorious.

"Your Grace," murmured the maid who met them on the landing. "The Duke of Storm would like to see you both before you retire for the night."

"Oh, husbands," said Juno. "Very well, if we must."

~

Cousin Henry inhabited the room that his mother the old Duchess always referred to as the cigar parlour. This was the place where gentlemen withdrew after dinner, seeking a respite from the company of female relatives. Such rooms generally held books, billiards and brandy… with an emphasis on the brandy.

Mneme had set foot in this particular cigar parlour once as a child, dared by Cousin Metis, but never as an adult. Juno appeared unsurprised at being drawn into such a masculine domain; clearly hers was a modern marriage.

"Come in, come in," called Henry cheerfully. He was arranged on an enormous sofa, which he shared with two of his hounds. A familiar bound edition rested on his lap: the same novel that had inspired tonight's so-called book club gathering. "Gad, this is a good book. Three ghosts, and twelve secret passages!"

"I'm glad someone's getting use of it," said Juno, leaning over to give him a careful kiss without disturbing the hounds. "Did you want to say good-night, my dear?"

"Ah, well," said Henry. "Thornbury had better explain."

Mneme looked up in surprise to see her favourite spell-cracker move from where he had been standing still, near the curtains.

"Goodness, you're tricksy," said Juno, putting a hand to her chest. "I didn't see you there at all!"

"A useful skill," said Mr Thornbury, exchanging a private nod with Mneme. She rather loved his quiet way of noting her presence, without fuss, when they met in the company of others. Still, he looked awfully serious tonight.

"What's wrong?" she asked.

Thornbury sighed. "A satirical print has been doing the rounds. And it may affect your campaign, Miss Seabourne. Rather catastrophically."

"Oh really," said Juno sharply. "As the lady who was the subject of rather a lot of 'Teacup Duchess' cartoons a few months ago, not to mention that dreadfully popular print depicting me as a buccaneer who stole Henry's heart, I rather think I am an expert on rising above such things. How bad could it be?"

Mneme had featured in some of those cartoons too, though mostly as part of a chorus of redheaded Seabourne witches. She had a sinking feeling that, from the look on her Thornbury's face, it was much worse than that.

"The print is about the portal campaign," Thornbury admitted. "But it doesn't feature either of you. It depicts the Queen."

PARLIAMENTARY QUESTION TIME

"*I*'m not sure we should be seen in public," said
Mneme. Embracing notoriety was one thing, but
as of yesterday she was a hair's breadth away from
treasonous.

"Nonsense," said Juno.

"It's not as if the story can become any *more* scandalous
at this point," said Lady Liesl, nibbling on a paper-thin
sandwich.

"That's hardly helpful," said Juno. "Some people aren't
built to absorb scandal. Look at Mneme, she's a wreck."

Mneme had been cursed with a stronger sense of
embarrassment than any other member of her family. Her
mother and aunts strode through the world as if they were
owed everything, and everyone around them was a lesser
being, unworthy of notice. If they liked something, it must
be fashionable. If they wanted something, it must be
available.

Juno and Liesl reminded her of the elder Seabournes;
despite their young age, the two ladies had enough confidence between them to match several wealthy matrons.
This in turn had bolstered Mneme's confidence, let her

believe that she could cast aside her old defences and act as a true Seabourne in public. Notorious and bold, letting no obstacle stand in the way of what she wanted to achieve.

Today, it was hard to remember why that had seemed like a good idea.

After a morning that attracted no calling cards to Storm Bolt (the first time this had ever happened with a Duchess in residence in the long history of the house), Juno decided they must go out to face the world. Mneme was worried that the word 'promenade' would be uttered… but even Juno could not argue with the new snowfall. Instead, her choice of venue in which to be seen was a splendid tearoom adjoining the grand edifice that was the Parliament of Gentles, at the heart of the Isle of Court.

The tea was strong, and the sandwiches a work of art.

Mneme would have preferred something further from the palace, given the circumstances. She rather suspected that Juno had grown addicted to all these sleigh rides back and forth across the frozen Scamander. Or perhaps she was simply delighted for a chance to wear all the different colours of fur stole that she had inherited along with the title of Duchess of Storm. Some of those furs must have been made at least four Duchesses ago, and they all smelled of expensive storage charms, which was to say of lavender and gently aged sandalwood.

Lady Liesl was easily convinced to join them. After her travels, following a dire month on her home estate with what sounded like a tragic number of dull cousins, she was hungry for proper society, even — especially, Mneme suspected during an uncharitable moment — in the midst of a royal scandal.

The cartoon, which had been widely distributed across the noble families of Town and Court with an efficiency that beggared belief, depicted Queen Aud of the Teatime Isles leaning out of a portal in a gentleman's boudoir: a brimming tankard in one hand, a military sword in the other, and a top hat upon her head. Her bosom spilled out of a tight waistcoat, as if she was a barmaid seeking a good time later.

The caption read: *What's Good Enough For the Lads Is Good Enough For Me.*

It made Mneme sick. Not only because it was crude and ugly, but because the joke turned on the idea that her portal campaign was ridiculous. She had done this. The Queen was a target for mockery because Mneme had dared to start a campaign about transportation convenience.

The joke was: we may be ruled by a woman, but we can still bring her low.

It wasn't funny, and yet all around Town and Court (and further, much further soon enough, it had been printed in two popular broadsheets and was likely already being sent north on postcards), men were sniggering at it.

The joke was: no woman is worthy of respect.

The joke was: Mneme's campaign was over before it had even started. No one would take the subject of portal travel for women seriously now.

"You need to stop thinking about it," Juno advised. "Changing the world is a long game. Catch your breath. Regroup."

"I think we should press ahead," Liesl said unexpectedly. "Honestly," and she dropped her voice slightly, clinking her teaspoon to prevent them being overheard, "Cutting that extra week off my travel here was liberating. Liberating! I don't care if I never step into another swan-shaped boat. What if we just started using portals as if it was usual? Duchess your way through it, Juno."

Juno hesitated, and Mneme knew she was thinking about that ugly cartoon. "There are already enough ladies at Court who think I'm a joke," she said quietly.

The dull fury that had been simmering in Mneme's stomach now rose up all of a sudden. "Wait, what? Who says that?"

"No one actually says it." Juno toyed with a cake, pasting on that bright, dazzling smile of hers. The one she always showed the world. "I'm a nobody who married well the first time around, and excellently the second time. Everywhere I go, there are those little looks and smiles and digs. I'm the social-climbing Duchess from a family no one's ever heard of. To these antique, generational old biddies, that means I'll never be worth the title."

"Balderdash," sputtered Liesl, who had picked up Juno's habit of swearing with Henry's vocabulary. She leaned back in the chair. "My dear Juno, you can't think…"

"Oh, you two," Juno said airily. "You're lovely. You especially, Liesl, since I caught the husband you were hunting. Mneme's nice to everyone."

"I'm really not," said Mneme. She felt miserable. All along, she had felt like she was imposing on Juno — the grand new Duchess, taking pity on her country cousin. It never occurred to her that Juno might be desperate for allies in this new life of hers.

"Look at what happened yesterday," Juno went on. "My first invitation to the Secret Senate, and see how the Countess and that Threnod woman completely ignored me?"

"That was my fault," said Mneme.

"It was not! Do you think they'd have spoken to you as they did if you were there with Henry's late mother? The real Duchess of Storm? No! They wouldn't have dared. If that Duchess wanted to travel by portal she'd have just… done it already, five times over, and hang the consequences."

Mneme didn't know whether to hug Juno or shake her.

"That Duchess of Storm was my aunt," she said quietly. "And — yes, she was magnificent at getting things done. People leaped to attention around her and cowered at her fury. But, uh. She wasn't very loveable."

Juno sagged with the first sign of bad posture Mneme had seen from her all winter. "I don't want to be loveable," she grumbled. "I want to be mighty and feared."

"I'm sorry," said Liesl in a careful voice, picking up a tiny cube of a rose cake with silver tongs. "Are you really complaining that being a Duchess isn't all it's cracked up to be? Is this the conversation we're having here, *your Grace*?"

Juno gave her a sharp look, and then burst into unexpected laughter. "Rich Duchess Problems," she giggled. "I should start an advice column for the newspapers."

"Is your Duke less than par?" Mneme joined in. "Bring him up to scratch with these three handy hints!"

The tension had eased. But it was not a conversation Mneme would soon forget.

"Sorry to interrupt," purred a voice. "But I've been longing to meet you, Miss Seabourne."

Mneme glanced around. The lady who had approached them — on her own, in a public tearoom, how daring — was what Cousin Metis would enviously describe as 'so extremely the mode.' Every inch of her was fashionable, like she had been printed on the front cover of *The Gentlewoman*, a lady's magazine full of fashion plates, cosmetic recipes and discreet employment advertisements.

She wore small sapphires, large pearls, and a gown so daringly up-to-the-minute with its slashed sleeves and jewel-toned ribbons that it must have been shipped from the Continent by express portal.

She had just come from outside, so still wore her exquisitely matching mantle in the deepest purple wool, and her bonnet: a startling artistic arrangement of basketry and floral artifice, so high that she might well be in danger from the candelabra if the ceilings were only a little lower. Her hair was twirled into dark ringlets that fell in an artful spiral beneath her hat and, Mneme had no doubt, would be charmed to stay perfect once the hat was removed.

"My dear, how lovely to see you," said Juno in a voice quite distant from the one she used with her actual friends. "Ladies, may I introduce you to Mrs Ceto Sevinny, wife of the Parliamentarian."

"Oh, we're all political wives around here," Mrs Sevinny said with a trilling laugh. "Even you, my dear."

"Lady Liesl of Sandwich," said Juno, smiling harder. "And Miss Mnemosyne Seabourne, of course."

"My dear, I do admire your work," gushed Mrs Sevinny. "Such daring and boldness."

"My work?" Mneme repeated.

"Your pamphlet, of course. Why, I have it here." She plucked it from her handbag, waving it gaily in their faces. "Quite the wittiest thing I've read in years and so true. I must confess I assumed you were a royalist, but now a certain print has been made public…" She lowered her voice a little, at least, as her sentence trailed into potentially treasonous territory. "Well, now I just know we can be friends."

Mneme stared at her, awash in the awkwardness of the situation. Had that cartoon really made people think that her stance on portals made her an anti-royalist? What on earth was she to say?

"When is your next meeting?" Mrs Sevinny demanded. "I can't wait to find out more about your campaign. Have you thought of extending it to the issues of the working woman, beyond the fripperies of the aristocracy?"

It was somewhat rich to hear that from a Parliamentarian's wife who was wearing enough fine tailoring and jewels to fund a dozen orphanages.

"Why, it's the day after tomorrow," broke in Juno. "I'll send a note along with the details. We must be discreet, after all."

This made Mrs Sevinny smile even more brightly than before. "Capital!" she exclaimed. "See you then!"

"Call a spellcracker," Liesl said dryly, as the most fashionable lady in town swished away. "Mneme has lost her voice."

"I couldn't think of a word to say to that woman," said Mneme, all astonishment at herself as much as the situation. "Goodness. Do you think everyone will think I'm out to topple the monarchy?"

"If you are, the Queen should watch out," Liesl said lightly. "I know how dangerous you can be, with a hedgehog in one hand and a teacup in the other."

"Why on earth did you tell her about the meeting?" Mneme asked Juno, once she had recovered somewhat from the encounter.

The Duchess of Storm sipped her tea. "We can send a maid later, tell her it's been called off for weather. If someone is ill-mannered enough to demand an invitation in person, the best thing to do is to let them think they've won for a little while."

"Or we can go ahead, hold a meeting and see how many other seditionist ladies want to join us," Liesl said thoughtfully. "Placard painting at eight, my dears, and corset-burning at ten of the hour."

A sound broke into their conversation: the discreetest possible clearing of an elderly throat. All three ladies turned in a single startle, wondering if Liesl's irreverent words had been heard.

Mrs Threnod stood there: a different kind of fashionable perfection, belonging to a long-faded era. She wore ruthless corsetry, the kind that Mneme's generation had thankfully been spared. When she stepped forward, there was a sad whispering sound as if the whales were mourning the loss of their bones. Her silver hair was pinned up under a bonnet so traditional that it belonged in an antique portrait of a terrifying ancestor, kept in the attic so as not to scare the children.

"Miss Seabourne," Mrs Threnod said stiffly. "My compliments to your mother. Will you take a turn with me about the gallery?"

Why not? Mneme thought wildly. *It's not like this day can get any stranger…*

"I'd be honoured," she said, and stood to take the old lady's arm. Beneath Mneme's gloved fingers, the arm felt as frail as a paper doll. "Need I fetch my hat?"

"Not at all," said Mrs Threnod. "We shan't be braving the weather."

So strange to think of Mrs Threnod as being the Countess of Balmady's companion; she seemed the kind of lady to have her own companion. A practical girl to wind her wool, read her lurid tales from the newspaper, and agree with her that the new temple priest wasn't a patch on the old one.

They walked up the spiral staircase that led from the tearoom up to an elegant open gallery, connecting to the domed building that housed the Parliament of Gentles. Other ladies were promenading here, admiring the fern fronds and hot-house roses kept alive by warming charms dotted around their large mosaic planters.

"Did you wish to speak on a private matter, Mrs Threnod?" Mneme asked. As the younger member of their party she was obliged to be twice as polite and encouraging.

"Indeed, madam. I suppose you're pleased with yourself, are you? Subjecting her Majesty to such a disgraceful situation."

Mneme breathed calmly. Managing cranky older ladies

was one of her regular family duties at home. She could handle this. "I don't believe I did anything to call her Majesty's attention to my campaign, nor to connect her publicly with it."

"You might as well have! I should say so."

"I did not draw nor distribute that disgraceful print, Mrs Threnod. Nor, come to that, did I distribute my pamphlets. They were stolen before I could collect them from the printer's."

"So you say," sniffed the disagreeable lady. "In any case, the whole shameful matter has made it very clear what must be done. I am sure you agree."

Mneme had missed something. "To what, exactly, am I agreeing?"

"Your portal campaign had a little merit," Mrs Threnod admitted reluctantly. "Bound for failure, of course, with such very young and unworldly girls leading the charge. It's an issue that the Great Discretion has been considering for a very long time, and so it's best you leave us to it."

Mneme stopped walking, and almost stumbled into a planter full of out-of-season rhododendrons, doing their best. "I'm sorry, you want to take over my campaign?"

"Not at all," said Mrs Threnod. "The very idea! We will, however, rescue the situation by replacing your weak and flawed campaign with a far superior model. By the end of the year, portals will be secured as a respectable mode of transportation for married women whose husbands and fathers are members of the Court of Lords. Have no doubt about it, young lady."

Married noblewomen. Of course.

"Perhaps in time, should the issue draw no further scandalous incident," Mrs Threnod mouthed the word 'scandalous' without letting the sound of it disrupt her sentence. "We might consider extending this honour to married ladies who have a connexion with the Parliament of Gentles."

"But no one else," said Mneme heavily. *Not even the Queen,* she thought in a sudden burst of insight. Queen Aud remained unmarried, despite many diplomatic attempts to secure her hand.

"Don't worry your head about it," said Mrs Threnod, in a pitying tone. "Best not corrupt an issue of such vital importance by associating it with your own family troubles, don't you think?" The word 'troubles,' like the word 'scandalous' was merely mouthed, not spoken aloud. "In the Countess of Balmady's hands, anything is possible."

Mneme wanted to cry or throw something. Instead, she circled back to Juno's table at the tearoom, releasing her grip on Mrs Threnod's arm. "You must do whatever you feel is best," she said to the older woman. "I'm sure you always do."

"Well!" said Mrs Threnod, looking exactly as offended as Mneme had intended her to be. To everyone's relief, she left it there.

Mneme dropped into the chair as they watched the Countess' companion sweep out of the tearoom. "I'm going to need more of that," she said, nodding at the cooling teapot. "And a great deal more cake."

OPERA CAN'T FIX EVERYTHING

"I have a solution to this entire mess," said Juno, as they made their way back across the river from the Parliament of Gentles.

It was a sign of ridiculous privilege to be tired of sleigh rides, but Mneme was sick and tired of this whole sorry winter. She did not think she could find a smile if one of the Frost Fair's legendary sword-swallowers leapt before her and downed a dozen scimitars without blinking.

"Go on," she said wearily as Thomas tucked them in with furs and blankets. If a thaw was coming soon, there was no sign of it today. "What is your brilliant solution?"

"The opera!" said Juno, as if pulling a dove out of her bonnet.

"No," said Mneme, and hoped that would settle the matter.

JUNO WAS STILL WHEEDLING when they returned home to Storm Bolt. The gentlemen had arrived ahead of them — by portal, of course — and were playing billiards in their shirt sleeves when Juno and Mneme invaded the cigar parlour.

Mneme's face was still stinging from the cold wind. She had torn the hem of her favourite winter dress when stepping out of the sleigh. It was quietly enraging to see how easily the men swooped about without having to worry about such things.

To Hades with portals. She was campaigning for trousers next.

Except of course, her campaign for portals was already a miserable failure.

Cousin Henry greeted his wife with a smacking kiss and a squeeze. Mr Thornbury, knowing that their usual discretion could be dropped in the presence of friends, relaxed enough to kiss Mneme's hand in greeting.

"Tell Mneme she's wrong," Juno barked.

"I couldn't possibly," said Thornbury with a secret smile. "It's so rarely the case."

Well, if he was going to say sweet things like that, Mneme could probably forgive him for the shirt sleeves.

"Opera," said Juno. "I think when life is strange and complicated, the best thing to do is go out and have a good time. Hence: the opera."

"That makes no sense to anyone that isn't you," Mneme argued. "I can't fuss about opera glasses all afternoon. I want to check on whether the Fenchurches have reprinted my pamphlets." She gave Juno a very stern look. "Since apparently we have a meeting coming up soon."

Juno was unabashed. "I have a wardrobe full of opera dresses you can borrow, and my maid is a genius with modiste charms to alter fittings, and the like. Thomas can check on your pamphlets later, while we're at the theatre. You're right to stay on top of this — we must make sure no one swoops in to steal your work again. Even if they did save you a lot of time by handing them out to society ladies…"

Mneme sighed, perching on Henry's reading couch. She wasn't going to sprawl all over it as he did. "Do you really think I should keep bothering?"

Thornbury brought her a cup of tea from the sideboard, where a teapot and light supper had been kept fresh with preservation charms, ready to be consumed at a moment's notice. "You're not losing confidence, are you?"

Mneme related the highlights of the conversations with Mrs Sevinny and Mrs Threnod. "It just all seems like such a mess," she finished. "Maybe I should keep my head down until this new scandal goes away… not to mention the old one. Let the Great Discretion bring in respectable portal travel for married ladies and hope that the rest will follow."

"And you'd be fine with that," said Thornbury. "A small change, when you could have been part of a mighty and glorious rebellion?"

"Rebellions destroy lives," said Mneme, leaning into his warmth. "I think everyone would be happier if I left it alone."

"I wouldn't!" called Juno from where she and her husband stood very close to each other, against the billiards table, with very little billiards being played. She giggled a little as Henry did something with his hands out of sight. "Really, Mneme. I'd make a splendid revolutionary."

"And become a social pariah?" It was all very well for Juno to be brave now, in front of her husband, as if she had not admitted to Mneme earlier today how much it might cost her.

"Hardly that."

"There were no calls this morning, Juno. You don't want to get on the wrong side of society just so I can score a point or two for equality."

"Stuff and nonsense," said Juno cheerfully. "The best thing to do is go out in public with our head held high, and show them all that their petty games can't affect us. I'm a Duchess, and no one is taking that away from me."

Mneme sighed again, more heavily than before. "Hence the opera?"

"Hence," said Juno, disappearing back into her husband's arms. "The opera!"

"Fine," said Mneme with a weary resignation. "The opera it is." She was here to be Juno's friend, above all things. If that meant the opera, then so be it.

APART FROM ANY other reason that Mneme might have wished to cry off, the Pantheon Opera House was on the Isle of Court which meant, once again, a sleigh ride across the ice.

Mneme was sure last time she spent any amount of time in Town, there was not the same kind of willy-nilly flitting back and forth across the Scamander. There were bridges, of course, and ferries for those who had no access to curricles or cabriolets. But still, a trip across the river was a rare treat, for those who had not negotiated themselves accommodation in Court apartments, or the palace itself.

Did Juno resent that her husband's town-house sat on this side of the river? Did she feel the need to make sure that Society remembered she was a Duchess now?

The gentlemen were chivalrous enough to join them in the sleigh this time, wrapped in great-coats and fur hats. Mneme found this slightly mollifying, while still being the absolute least they could do.

The Pantheon was very grand, with five tiers of galleries arching up into a peaked roof that looked like Mrs

Sevinny's bonnet. The fashion these days was for even the very grandest of patrons to occupy the pit, so as to be properly seen by everyone else from their progressively cheaper seats, up into the heavens.

Mneme, with this in mind, had chosen one of Juno's less extravagantly daring gowns for the evening, and paired the green velvet with a lace fichu which may well have belonged to one of her great-grandmothers.

Juno rolled her eyes at Mneme's choice, complaining that she might at least wear the family pearls if she was going to dress like a maiden aunt. Cousin Henry, however, seemed to approve. "Don't want you catching the muslin disease, eh, Mneme?" he guffawed. "All these pretty young things wandering around risking colds and the winter lung to look dainty."

Marriage, Mneme considered, had somehow transformed Cousin Henry from a cheerful young buck in his late twenties to a middle-aged uncle out of a comic novel. Still, he was happier than she had seen him in years.

Tonight's opera was a recent production by an up-and-coming composer, featuring the very popular castrato Hermes Fiero (a stage name if ever Mneme had heard one), a handsome young man with a horde of devoted fans who printed entire publications of love letters to his boyish face and could often be spotted following him around in public groups and giggling behind their hands.

It was the sort of thing that made Mneme desperately glad that she did not have younger sisters. Her sense of personal embarrassment was challenged enough. Bad enough to overhear Lady Liesl and Juno making sly comments to each other about the tight fit of his trousers.

The custom in the theatre was for a mixed group to sit male-female where possible, like a dinner party, but that arrangement did not suit Juno at all. She preferred to be gossiping with her ladies. Every time there was an intermission (this particular opera had at least six), she was up and moving everyone around into a different configuration.

Mneme noticed that Henry and Thornbury ended up seated next to each other more often than not, falling into secret conversations together. Henry had brought a school chum of his, Figgy, to make up the numbers. Juno disapproved of any attempts to set Figgy and Liesl up together, which mean more often than not that Mneme ended up wedged in next to that particular gentleman. Figgy's idea of intelligent conversation with ladies was pretty much limited to "Splendid night, what?" which at least did not require much in the way of a response.

The music was pleasant enough. The opera house blazed in full lights throughout — old fashioned candelabra instead of charms — so Mneme was able to read the libretto when she tired of gazing soulfully at the star of the show.

Juno was correct that *simply everyone* was at the opera tonight. Mneme spotted many people she knew, including the beautifully dressed Mr and Mrs Sevinny. By some accident, they were seated rather too close to the Count and Countess of Balmady, which caused quite a few uncomfortable looks back and forth.

Mr Thornbury, Mneme noticed, paid particular attention to this part of the audience, even when the music was at its most dramatic.

"Do you have a professional interest in this opera?" she teased him when the next intermission switched them around again, so they were sitting together.

He gave her a guarded look. "What on earth do you mean by that?"

Surprised at the intensity of his response, she sought to lighten the mood. "What professional interest might a spellcracker have in a place like this? Operatic sabotage, of course."

He relaxed, with a smile so warm that she felt the velvet of her gown heating up, rather. "Rival castrati setting traps for each other on stage? Hexes in the costume box…"

"Wax dollies in the stage furnishings," she teased back. "Love charms in the curtain cords…"

Thornbury paid attention to her for the rest of the evening, which on the whole made the opera more enjoyable than Mneme had expected.

"Thomas, did you collect Miss Seabourne's parcel?" Juno asked as they poured out of the opera house many hours later. It had been snowing, with fresh coats of white layered on every street and rooftop. Thomas had a slight dusting of whiteness on his own heavy coat, from where he had been waiting for them to emerge.

"I'm afraid not, your Grace," said Thomas, as he handed them all into the sleigh and pulled out the blankets and furs. "The printer's tent was closed when I arrived."

"Already?" said Juno, put out. "Goodness. Can they have run out of those little cards that were so popular?"

"Surely the point of printing them on the ice is that they don't run out," said Henry.

"I asked around a bit, and they were closed all day," volunteered Thomas. "I tried having a nose around inside, your Grace, in case Miss Seabourne's papers were out where they could be seen. But a watchman came past and I had to scarper right quick."

"Good show," said Juno. "Mrs Fenchurch got her value from that bribe, then."

"I hope she's all right," Mneme said worriedly, as the

sleigh set off. Last time they spoke to Mrs Fenchurch, she had sounded determined to spend every minute she could working the crowds at the fair.

Juno snorted. "That depends, doesn't it? If her printing press was behind that royal hatchet job, she's done well to lie low."

"You think the Fenchurches published that awful cartoon about the Queen?" Mneme said in surprise.

"What else can Sevinny have been about?"

"Wait," said Thornbury abruptly. "Did you say Sevinny commissioned that print?"

"We don't know that," Mneme said quickly. It made a lot of sense, though. "He did commission the Fenchurches for *a* satiric print. By a friend of his, he said. Around the same time as my pamphlets."

"I wouldn't be surprised if that wretched fellow took your pamphlets too," said Juno firmly. "His wife ended up with a copy, after all. I'm sure she could have lent him a maid to play that trick."

Thornbury exchanged a look with Henry that Mneme did not understand, though she filed it away to think about later. What interest could the two of them possibly have in the Parliamentarian's activities?

"You know what?" Henry said a moment later, as their sleigh reached the apartments where Lady Liesl was staying. "Never mind this going home business. There could be a thaw any day now. Let's enjoy the Frost Fair while we can."

"Oh, yes!" said Liesl, clapping her hands. "I want to buy souvenirs for my sisters. What's the point of being in Town when something exciting happens, if not to lord it over all the relatives who are missing out on the fun?"

"Capital idea," said Thornbury, and his hand, beneath layers of blanket, found Mneme's and squeezed it gently. "I heard they brought in an elephant to walk upon the ice. Don't want to miss that."

"I imagine the elephant would have preferred to stay home in the warm," said Mneme tartly, but she allowed him to keep holding her hand.

THIN ICE

Walking on the ice among the tents and stalls allowed Mneme the opportunity to take Mr Thornbury's arm and speak privately with him. It was an age since they had been anything like alone with each other.

"We are going to investigate the printer's tent, aren't we?" she asked him. "Just you and me."

"Of course we are," he replied in a low voice. "Unless you'd prefer we arrange for a chaperone?"

Mneme nestled her arm more tightly into his. With the bright lights and flames around them, and so many people, hardly anyone would pay them attention — and Juno and Henry, those most likely to note their absence, not only approved of their match but had been actively encouraging it.

"I suppose you *are* going to marry me," she said archly.

"Name the day." Thornbury sounded entirely earnest, which took Mneme's breath away. Unless that was the chill from the ice beneath their feet.

"I think it vital to inform you as my future husband

that I expect to be invited on all mysterious midnight adventures," she informed him.

Thornbury nodded gravely. "You'll have to invest in a black stocking cap and harlequin mask. To ensure discretion."

"I'll consult my seamstress in the morning!"

Their group stopped for ices at a stall. Mneme was already chilly and would have preferred a hot toddy of some sort, but Henry's friend Figgy made a palaver about new flavours that had to be tasted to be believed.

The dishes of ice were handed around: black tea, punch water, rye bread and muscadine. Mneme let the others choose first, which meant she ended up with parmesan when she would have much preferred royal cream or pineapple. Joke was on everyone: hers was delicious, and frozen into the shape of a mouse, which she found rather amusing.

Juno ate a bright red barberry ice, frozen into the shape of an anarchist's bomb. "Start as one means to go on!" she said gaily as she licked her spoon.

The circus was stationed near the Tethys bridge, drawing such crowds that Mneme swore she could feel the ice creaking under her feet. In any case, what with the dancing bear, the flame jugglers and the tumbling clowns, it was easy enough to drift aside from their main party.

Thornbury's gloved hand was firm and warm around Mneme's as he tugged her away from their friends, behind a fortune teller's tent and into the darkness. They stepped lively along a channel formed by many tents backing up against each other, careful not to trip over pegs and ropes.

Actually, how did one secure a tent on the ice? Mneme looked down to see, but Thornbury's arm urged her on. He was remarkably cheerful about their mission. Perhaps, like her, he was sick of polite society.

It felt like they were off on an adventure together, in

their own little world. Thornbury kept glancing at Mneme to check she was still there beside him, though their arms remained tangled together. Each time, his smile creased up a little more.

They paused some while later, behind the thick slats of a hut that must have been built very recently. Carpenters, at least, were still finding work during the great frost. "Are we close?" Mneme asked, but when Thornbury turned to look at her, the expression on his face left her breathless again.

They had kissed before, here and there. They had learned to choose their moments, ducking around chaperones and Duchesses and other obstacles. But they had never quite kissed like this before.

Thornbury pressed Mneme against the back of the hut and captured her with his mouth. *No one* had never kissed her like this before. A few shy courtship rituals that came to nothing, with gentlemen who had not suited. Thornbury himself had always been so careful with her reputation, knowing that even the occasional moment of *alone* was an illusion, in houses full of other people.

They were not alone now. Even as Mneme felt the heat of him pressing through the layers of their clothes, and the rough scrape of the creaky hut at her back, she could hear chatter and murmurs, of the Frost Fair vendors and patrons. The air was full of flute music and happy shouts.

Was it even winter? She had never felt so overdressed in her life.

Thornbury's mouth was a revelation, all propriety cast aside. Mneme kissed him back as passionately as she knew how, and learned a few new things into the bargain. Mostly, what to do with one's hands at a time like this.

Finally, they drew apart. Thornbury remained relentlessly close, his face pressed tenderly into the softest part of her throat. An ache rolled through Mneme like a shiver, slow and sensuous.

He drew back from her, a few seconds later. The spell was broken, and the polite veil of the gentleman fell back over his demeanour. Thornbury opened his mouth to speak.

Mneme cut him off. "Don't you dare apologise."

Her eyes had adjusted enough to this shadowy, makeshift alley that she saw his face crease once more into a smile. Her favourite smile in the world. One that she claimed possession of, entirely. "I wouldn't dream of it," said Thornbury, and gave her the kind of familiar caress — a hand to the hip, a brief squeeze — that reminded her of how Henry and Juno were together, still newly married and enchanted with each other. "I do think, however," he went on. "We might return to our friends with the news of an engagement rather than an understanding?"

"I suppose it will give me something to write to my mother about," Mneme said with a mock-sigh. "But first — breaking and entering?"

"Breaking and entering," he agreed happily, as if she had given him a gift.

THE PRINTER'S tent remained closed, with a lock and chain on the front, and a damp sign saying *Back for Business Soon* which had clearly survived more than one patter of snow.

"Do you know what bulk and file means?" Thornbury asked as the two of them strolled along the ice together, pausing by the glass-blower's stand next door. Mneme was easily distracted by the beautiful artistry as the glass-blower created a gleaming, impossible ball with a hare inside, coloured pale pink and white. She could not sense any use of magic at all. Pure craft and technical skill.

"That particular phrase wasn't taught at my finishing school," she replied.

Thornbury leaned into her, his breath warm on her cheek. "The bulk keeps watch while the file picks the pocket," he said quietly.

"That had better not be your way of telling me to keep watch while you have all the fun!"

The spellcracker hesitated, and she could see he was torn. "Wait five minutes, then join me around the back," he decided finally, and squeezed her arm one more time before hurrying away, apparently in the opposite direction.

Mneme waited, watching the glass-blower swirl a galaxy of snowflakes inside a bauble. His stall was scattered with printed labels that read *Made on the Ice*, ready to be attached to the new pretties. Perhaps, on another day, she could return and purchase a gift for her mamma. Something suitably grand to suggest that, while Mneme was never going to marry a Duke or anyone who might qualify for the Court of Lords someday, she could still give Mrs Galatea Seabourne something to brag about at parties.

Mneme moved on, joining the crowd past the next few stalls. She stepped aside to let a large family pass, sharing a bag of hot chestnuts that she envied greatly, and slid herself into the space between two tents.

She doubled back quickly, counting canvases, until she came up to the heavy sailcloth, treated with tar and polish, which belonged to the printer's hut.

Someone — Thornbury, she assumed — had already slit the seam of the tent carefully at one corner, all the way down. It was only noticeable with a heavy breeze and hopefully would not catch the eye of the diligent watchman who had sent Thomas the driver packing.

Mneme curled her fingers around the sailcloth and eased it aside, slipping into the musty darkness. The damp air smelled like metal and paper. The flap fell closed behind her, leaving them in darkness.

"Be still," Thornbury hissed. "Make a light."

Silently, Mneme cast a small glowing lantern into her palm, one of the first charms she had learned at her mamma's knee. It looked like the head of a dandelion, with thousands of white pin-pricks glowing over her skin; it always came out that way, even when she tried to form fancier lantern charms.

It was bright enough to reveal Mr Thornbury, frozen in the centre of the room, his hands outstretched and still.

As her eyes adjusted to the light, Mneme saw the scene more deeply. He held dozens of fine strands of magic in place, spiralling outwards. She had learned to see through the eyes of a spellcracker when they worked together at Henry's country estate, during the events of Last Season. In truth, this had always been a skill she worked at; when your mother was a Seabourne, and thus one of the most powerful and skilled enchantresses in the Teacup Isles, you learned to spot traps.

There were traps here. Mneme watched them unfold before her eyes; they were all ensnared in Thornbury's web, but still poised and ready to fall upon his head.

"I only saw the one at first," he said between gritted teeth. "A hairline hex, easy to pluck away. And another beneath it. I thought that was all. Stay back, whatever you do. Stay in contact with the wall of the tent."

Thornbury dissolved one hex and caught the next, working slowly backwards. It was a triple cavalcade, Mneme realised. He had cracked one security spell and set off three more, which in turn sparked three more each.

"Why would a printer have this breadth of magical protection?" she wondered aloud. The spell was twice as complex as anything she had seen at the private houses of the highest aristocracy.

"Fenchurch wasn't just a printer," said Thornbury. *Snap, snap, snap*. One by one, he separated the threads of the hex and destroyed them, while holding all the others in place. He was sweating.

Chalk sigils appeared on the floor, forming a circle that encompassed Thornbury and the printing press. He began erasing them, one by one, with whispered words. Each seemed to cause him a jolt of pain.

"Wasn't," Mneme repeated. There was a dark, odd shadow sticking out from beneath the printing press. A shadow with arms, and legs. "Oh gods, is that a body? Is that Mr Fenchurch?"

"No," said Thornbury in a flat sort of voice. "It's not." There was a sizzling sound as a thread of the spell trap flicked free of his control, running across the pleated ceiling. He caught it with a strand of magic from his little finger, and groaned with the effort. "This is an Arachne master hex," he told her. "Royal security level. And like a fool, I thought I could handle disarming it because *I know all the passwords*."

Mneme blinked. That was a lot of information. Not all of it made sense yet. "But you don't in fact know all the passwords?"

"Apparently not," he said, and for a moment his eyes met hers. He was breathing heavily. "I'm sorry, Mneme."

"What's that supposed to —" she started to say, but the remaining chalk sigils burst into flame. Thornbury let out a short breath, and the threads of magic around him snapped all at once.

The ice cracked under his feet, and then disappeared entirely, dropping Mr Thornbury, the printing press and the unnamed corpse directly into the freezing waters of the River Scamander.

As the daughter of one of the oldest magical families in living memory, Mneme was taught as a very young child that kidnap was inevitable.

From the moment she first began to show sparks of magical ability, her tutors were told to take this into account. They duly taught her all kinds of ladylike responses to emergency, including a trilling bell sound and a charm to drop magical 'breadcrumbs' which would allow her to be efficiently rescued by the authorities.

One summer, when her mamma and aunts had their heads bent together over some sorcerous plot or other at the Seabourne family home, Mneme and her cousins were put under the charge of Henry's latest tutor.

Lars Zephyr was younger than the usual breed of tutors: a slender man made haggard before his time. He had a face like a lightly warmed-up skull, and the ethics of a pirate.

"Honour is for thieves and corpses," he told the children in that flat voice of his. "No one expects children of the nobs to be ruthless or vicious. No one will expect anything of you at all but a reedy squeal and a bit of sobbing. Being underestimated is your best weapon."

Mr Zephyr taught them to find a place of deep anger and pain within them, and connect it to every magic charm or hex or curse they'd ever known. He hunted them through the corridors of Shellwich Standing and leaped out at them from trees and shrubberies. Once, memorably, he set them running along the beach for hours, believing themselves pursued, only to leap out at them from behind a sandcastle once they thought the exercise was over.

Henry thought the whole thing was brilliant and hilarious. Even now, he could produce fireworks and stampeding elephant sounds when someone gave him a shock without warning. Cousin Metis was a slower student, but eventually unpacked enough ladylike rage to absorb the lessons. Mr Zephyr was pleased by her progress.

Mneme had been unsettled by the whole idea. Her childhood with a dramatic and sometimes unstable mamma had taught her to turn her frustration inward. When surprised, her reaction was usually somewhere between sarcasm and asking too many questions, both of which were hard to weaponise.

She knew she was a frustrating student. Eventually, Mr Zephyr took her aside while the others built emergency flares and explosives out of ordinary household objects.

"You're a talented kid," he said gruffly. "But cleverness with words isn't everything. You need to find some place deep inside yourself where you don't care how you look to others, or what they think of you. You need to let yourself to react in a real emergency. Get loud. Get messy. Get mean. That is the only way to keep yourself alive when every second counts. *React*."

Before tonight, Mneme had only needed to use that advice when playing the New Croquet with other ladies.

But, she had to admit, it had been terribly helpful for that. And also, for this.

~

Every second counts.

Mneme stood frozen for a whole second after Thornbury fell through the ice. And then she reacted.

Mr Zephyr would have been proud of her. She wasn't thinking at all. She let her magic do the panicking.

She exploded.

The tent went flying up above her, slashed to ribbons. Lights and sound flared from her fingers. Around her, she saw a whirl of unexpected transformations spiral outwards. The glassblower's animals came to life and danced in a parade before her eyes: pot-bellied pigs, and kittens, and hedgehogs. Of course, there were hedgehogs.

"HELP!" she screamed. Her magic bled into the sound, amplified it.

Help came running in the form of watchmen and stallholders. Mneme didn't need to say anything — the yawning pit of broken ice spoke for itself.

"Icebreak!" hollered some. Others dropped back to steer worried patrons away from the danger area.

"How many down there?" the nearest watchmen yelled.

"One man," Mneme gasped. "No, two." The thought of rescuers dredging up whomever was dead under the printing press and leaving Thornbury down there was beyond the pale.

They had a practiced routine for these situations — and they all knew the rules. Magic users came forward quickly, joining hands and sending light probes into the deep water, flickering darts. Others gathered blankets at the ready.

"Flipping printing press," one of them muttered. "Should be banned. Might as well bring on the blinking elephants."

A woman from the cider stall drew Mneme aside, and wrapped an extra coat around her shoulders. Mneme realised that she was shaking, her teeth chattering wildly. She tried to raise a charm to warm her hands, and came up empty — she had poured every scrap of magic into her warning cry. It would take time to recover her energy. No wonder she felt like falling asleep on her feet.

"They're good at this," the cider-wife assured her. "Is he magic, your man?"

Is he magic? Mneme wanted to laugh. Wanted to explain to the woman about that last tendril of a charm Thornbury had thrown at her, securing her against the tent wall even as he fell.

"He is," she managed.

"He's got the best possible chance, then."

It felt like hours passed, though it was only a few minutes before the crumpled figure of Mr Thornbury, dripping and limp, was hoisted up out of the hole in the ice.

"Savage break," muttered one of the helpers. "Lucky it was contained."

The last threads of Thornbury's self-protection spell snapped as his feet hit solid ice. Mneme stumbled to him, but the efficient volunteers were a wall between them. She had to let them help — they had warming charms at their disposal, while she had nothing but exhausted panic and cold hands.

"Not too much," the cider-wife called out. "Easy there, Eamonn. Gotta thaw him slow, or he'll end up with charcoal for skin. Get them to the Pickled Pear," she added to the volunteers who had come forward with a sledge. "I'll see them right."

"Everyone's so kind," Mneme whispered, her cheeks stinging as she helped a shuddering Thornbury into the sledge and tucked blankets around him.

"You get in with him," the cider-wife urged. She set her own warming charms on three points of the top-most blanket. "Keep it steady there. We look after our own on the ice," she added. "Dangerous way to make a living, and it does none of us any good when there are fatalities." Her face darkened and she darted a look behind her, where the volunteers had pulled another body out of the ice. "Looks like they couldn't save the other one."

It would probably not be a good idea to tell the woman that the other man was already dead when he hit the water. Mneme kept her mouth shut as she slid on to the sledge next to Thornbury, under the layers. "The Pickled Pear?"

"That's my place. Get him in a hot bath for a bit and set hot bricks in the bed — that'll do a better job overnight than any amount of magic. My Elsie's there, tell her Luce sent you. She'll know what to do." The cider-wife huffed impatiently, looking up at the sky as snow began to fall softly around them. "Look at that. Could have used it an hour ago to shore up the ice and stop this sort of thing happening, couldn't we just?"

The last thing Mneme saw as they were dragged away across the ice by two burly volunteers was the glass-blower. He raced around frantically, chasing the runaway glass animals that had been affected by Mneme's panic flare. They were a lot larger than before she unleashed her magic… and far more of them were hedgehogs than had previously been the case.

On a normal night, Mneme would be mortified at causing so much trouble. Right now, all she could do was hang on to Mr Thornbury and be grateful that he had survived.

~

WORD TRAVELLED AHEAD OF THEM. They were greeted at the Pickled Pear (a docklands pub, overlooking the frozen river and bearing a sign that said *YES WE ARE OPEN, COME FROSTE OR SNOW. ASKE ABOUT OUR SPICED CIDER!*

Elsie was every bit as generous and comforting a presence as her wife. She bundled the two of them into a room upstairs with a burning fire and a giant tin bath with a warming charm set under it.

"We can pay," Mneme assured her. "We, uh, work for the Duke of Storm." She did not feel the need to throw around more airs and graces than that.

"I can't spare anyone to send word to your people," Elsie warned. "Not till closing, and maybe not then if this snow gets any thicker."

"It's fine," said Mneme. Everyone involved in all this had assumed she and Thornbury were married, and she didn't want anyone separating them now out of misplaced propriety. She could send a paper bird to Juno once her magic recharged, if the Duchess hadn't already heard the story on the Frost Fair grapevine. "What should I do now?"

"Bath first," said Elsie briskly. "The bricks are in the bed. Will you be wanting a healing draught?"

Mneme wanted to say that she could handle it herself, but she didn't have more than a spark left in her right now. Besides, healing charms had never been her specialty. "That would be very kind."

"As you like. See you dry him off good and well, get him into bed and hop right in there beside him. Keep an eye out for any parts going blue but it's his innards you need to protect most of all. My draught will help with that."

"You must have seen a few of these cases over the

years," Mneme said, already stripping Thornbury of his sodden coat and shirt. His eyes were half-open, but he hadn't said a word since they pulled him out of the water. He was usually a quiet, watchful sort of person, but this level of silence from him was unnerving. Clearly, he was concentrating all his energy on not being dead.

"Here's where they bring 'em if anyone goes into the drink," said Elsie. "One Frost Fair, years ago, we had a whole circus through here at one point. Elephants have no place on the ice," she added darkly. "That's just asking for the gods to have a poke. You need help getting your man undressed?"

"I can do it," Mneme said quickly.

"I'll leave you, then. Cider to pour. Sing out if you have any worries. I'll put a bowl of soup outside the door when I have a minute." She dropped a wink at Mneme as she bustled out the door. "I'll make sure to save the bill for that Duke of yours, don't you worry about that."

MNEME HAD IMAGINED spending time with Mr Thornbury without his clothes, once they were married. She had expected it would be a far more joyous occasion. Instead, she stripped him in a business-like fashion and helped him into the warm water, which didn't feel nearly warm enough.

Thornbury sighed with something like satisfaction as he was engulfed in the water. Finally, he opened his eyes properly and looked at her like he recognised her. "You're good in a crisis," he mumbled through cracked lips.

Mneme laughed and almost burst into tears. "I'm *loud* in a crisis. And terribly good at having people rush to my rescue."

"Don't knock it if it works."

She let him soak for as long as she dared. When it looked like he might fall asleep, she drew him out and towelled him off, drying his hair and limbs. (She put her maidenly modesty aside to towel the parts in between, looking firmly at his face the whole time.)

It was a small room with a big bed, designed for bundling. You could fit a couple of families in here, if needs be. Mneme collected a covered dish that Elsie had placed outside the door, and two flasks: a small healing draught, and a much larger flask of warm cider with spices. She helped Thornbury to swallow his draught and a spoonful or two of soup, then helped herself to her own supper. She was ravenous.

How ridiculous that the last things they had eaten together were ices.

Finally, Thornbury leaned back on the faded pillow and sighed into sleep. He was already a better colour than when they first arrived.

Mneme had blushed enough for one day. She took another deep swallow of cider, pulled off her layers of mantle, gown and stockings, until she only had the last whisper of a petticoat left. Then she lifted the heavy covers and joined her future husband in bed.

Her job tonight was to keep him warm.

It was many hours before the sounds and rattle-thumps from the cider-house quietened. Mneme slept a little, though she kept startling awake, feeling the need to check that the covers were properly tucked around Mr Thornbury's feet.

She lit a candle at one point, resenting that her worn-out magic could not be trusted to produce even a dab of light. From the flickering orange glow of the candle, she determined that his hands and feet had not suffered too badly from the exposure to the icy river.

Next time she awoke, she was far warmer than she had ever been in her life. Thornbury was plastered to her, heat rolling off his skin. No need for more bricks after all. She stroked his hair, and he turned his face gently into the soft hollow of her throat, as he had earlier that night after kissing her in such a spectacular fashion.

Mneme let her breath out very slowly. "Can you move your hands?" she whispered.

"Why, Miss Seabourne," he said in a voice animated enough to sound teasing. "I never."

"In this room, I'm Mrs Thornbury, thank you very much," she said tartly. "It wasn't a proposition, my dear. I need to check for frostbite."

He moved his fingers. As both hands were currently pressed against her, she felt them through her exceptionally thin petticoat.

"My dear," he mumbled. "Like the sound of that."

Of course, they both fell asleep again before anything more interesting could happen.

~

THE NEXT TIME MNEME AWOKE, it was to find the fire freshly banked, a teapot on the bureau beside her, and her future husband pulling on a fresh set of woollen socks.

"I don't know who you told the landlady we are," he said, turning his head to her. "But she is remarkably confident we'll be paying our bill."

"I dropped Henry's name," Mneme admitted, pushing herself up on her elbows. As the blankets slid down, Thornbury's eyes were drawn to her. Not *all* business this morning, then. "I hope that's all right," she said, and let the blankets slide a little lower. No use pretending she was not a scandalous creature now.

"Absolutely it is. I need to speak to him as soon as possible. Might be difficult." He nodded to the curtained window. "Snow fell high last night. Our cider-wife hosts are serving breakfast to volunteers who are willing to shovel a path, but they can't start until the snow stops… and it hasn't yet."

"Can't you use magic to send word?" Mneme asked. "A paper pigeon won't survive a snowstorm, but the weather shouldn't affect scrying." She hesitated, loathe to admit to him that he might have to do it, as she wasn't sure any spells would work for her right now, even after a good night's sleep. "I'm sure they have a portal for travellers."

"What?" Thornbury said with a small smile. "And leave you here in a cider-house with strangers? I'm not that much of a bounder. I sent several messages this morning already," he added, nodding to a half-full teacup abandoned near the mantle. "Scrying, and other charms. But it's still early, and I don't know if Henry or anyone else I tried to reach will be awake yet."

"You don't think Cousin Henry and Juno will have spent the night scouring the Frost Fair to find out what happened to us?" Mneme was only half serious.

Thornbury winced. "I rather think they'll assume I whisked you off to have my wicked way with you at last. Knowing Henry, he probably covered for us a little too well."

"If he didn't, Juno probably did," Mneme sighed. "If only our friends thought we had higher morals."

He laughed, and then coughed with a dry and scraping sound that made her heart hurt.

Mneme slid out of the blankets, the floor a cold hard shock against her bare feet. What she should do is pull on her respectable garments, but she was compromised the moment they were left alone in this bedroom together. What difference would a few more minutes make? She went straight to him, flung her arms around his shoulders and said, "I thought you were *dead*."

"Me too, for a minute." Thornbury kissed her hair. "Much though I would love to savour this impromptu honeymoon, I have to report what happened at the printer's tent, as soon as possible."

"Report to whom?" Mneme frowned.

"To the Queen, if I can."

"The *Queen*?"

"Darling, I'm sorry, but I can't explain everything, not yet."

Darling. She liked the sound of that. The rest of it was most unsettling. Last time they collaborated on a grand adventure, they had been partners with an equal stake in the outcome. Right now, she didn't even know what game they were playing. What sort of marriage could they make if Thornbury didn't trust her when it was important?

"Can you tell me who was dead under the printing press? Not Mr Fenchurch, you said. But I'm sure it was a man."

Mneme would have wept buckets already if she thought the brittle, sparky Mrs Fenchurch had met such an unfortunate end.

"I'm rather afraid," said Mr Thornbury gravely. "That was Galbreath Sevinny."

FIGHT OR FLIGHT

"Sevinny," said Mneme, horrified. "But he was at the opera last night. We saw him."

"Indeed," said Thornbury. He nodded to her. "Dress quickly, please. This view is charming, but we don't have a lot of time."

Mneme pulled on her gown and stockings as swiftly as she could. Velvet in the daytime felt ridiculous, but at least it was warm. "Because of all the snow shovelling we have to do?"

"No," said Thornbury, looking pained. "Because there *is* a portal in this inn, and I just felt someone break every security measure placed upon it. Not gently."

Someone yelled, downstairs, and there was the sound of shattering glass.

"The roof," Thornbury said swiftly. "Are those all your clothes?"

Despite her fingers trembling on the buttons, Mneme had managed to put on several layers of petticoat, opera gown, and gloves. Her boots were drying by the fire, and she pulled those on now, lacing them quickly. It was a good thing she had learned to do without a maid, thanks to her mamma constantly monopolising the staff on their home estate. "I had a mantle," she reminded him. "And you had an overcoat. But they were stripped off us when we first came into the cider-house." Hopefully, Elsie and Luce had secured the garments somewhere they could dry off, without being pinched by other customers. "I'm sorry, did you say the roof?"

More crashing downstairs, and more shouting.

"Are we under attack?" Mneme demanded. "Mr Thornbury, you can't drag me on to a roof without explaining!"

"If I promise to explain later, will you come without question?" he begged.

But, the roof.

"You nearly drowned yesterday," she said plaintively.

Thornbury held his hand out to her. "No one ever drowned on a roof."

"If you give me a moment to think about it, I'm sure I can challenge your claim!"

Their room was high, with a pointed gable roof overlooking the street — but not as high as it used to be. The snow had banked up deep overnight. Mneme could see thick channels down the centre of the street where someone had powered through with a plough or intensive fireball, but the lower floors of all the buildings overlooking the river were snowed in, up to their first row of windows.

She could not see any way up to the roof from here, and did not dare prod her magic to see if she had enough left to cushion her fall if she slipped. She would have to rely on those snowbanks being softer than they looked.

There was a whistle from the roof above. Mr Thornbury, balancing precariously on the window ledge, let out a matching whistle. A rope ladder spiralled down, falling past their ledge. Not long enough to reach the ground, but certainly a leg up in reaching the roof. "You first," said

Thornbury, holding the ladder steady. "Quick as you can. Whomever smashed through that portal just now is likely after us."

Mneme climbed on to the rope ladder. This, at least, she could manage. She and her cousins once spent a whole summer perfecting the art of the treehouse. "How did you manage this?" she called down to him once she reached the slippery, snow-laden roof tiles. There were several patches without snow at all, as if someone had been up here recently. Someone in big boots.

Thornbury untied the rope ladder at the top and made it disappear into a pocket. Clearly his own magic had not suffered from the incident in the river. "One of my messages must have got through."

Mneme wanted to know to whom he had been sending messages. That wasn't all she wanted to know. She was so full of questions she might burst.

Thornbury cast some kind of charm on her boots, and Mneme almost immediately felt steadier, less likely to slip and fall. "Now we run," he told her. "Fast. Imagine this is a game of croquet, and someone will make you marry a gregarious Baron if you lose."

"Are you trying to get us killed?"

"Not in the least. My faith in your croquet skills is exceptionally high."

They ran, hand in hand, across snow-laden roof tops. This was the kind of street where every roof touched the nearest building, so they were able to make it quite far until a nearby chimney exploded into sparks.

Thornbury grabbed Mneme around her waist and pulled her down behind another chimney.

"Did someone just shoot at us with a musket?" she demanded. "A *musket*?"

"I imagine so. A fireball would have done more damage, and this doesn't smell like any battle-hex I know."

Thornbury scooted down the roof to a balcony. He drew Mneme with him, sliding off the snow-damp awning to crouch beneath it. "Down to ground level, I think, snow or no snow."

They tumbled down a rackety set of outdoor stairs into a courtyard full of uneven snowdrifts. An archway leading to the street was only half-full of snow, allowing them to crawl over and through.

Now Mneme's knees were wet and freezing. She had never wanted warming charms so much in her life. Also, trousers.

"Why are people after us?" she asked as they clambered out into a smaller alley, one that was part-roofed and thus had bald patches instead of solid snow all through it.

"You agreed not to question me until later," said Thornbury.

"I have been remarkably restrained!"

"Fine." Holding her hand again, he peered out to the street behind, looking both ways, and then tugged her along with him. This street had a walkway that had been cleared and salted. "I don't know why they're after us. This sort of thing tends to happen, though, when we get close."

"To each other?" That seemed a bizarre presumption for him to make.

"When we get close to figuring out what's going on."

"And what *is* going on?" More to the point, though this was a question she did not dare ask, what did 'we' mean to him, if not including herself?

"I'll tell you when I figure it out!"

There was a piercing whistle, like the one from earlier.

Across the street, a man in black waved at them from the driving seat of a coach and horses. He wore a hood, and his face was covered with a tied cloth, so that he looked like a bandit.

"Our pursuers have grown friendly," Mneme remarked.

"That one actually is a friend," said Thornbury. "Most days."

They dodged a couple of crowded carriages as they ran across the cleared part of the road. Mneme found herself bundled into the coach on her own, much to her dismay, while Thornbury threw himself up on to the box with the coachman.

"I'll just be thinking up more questions from in here!" she yelled through the window.

There was a snort of a laugh that came from both men.

Their carriage ride ended at the Niobe Bridge; closed thanks to the night's heavy snowfall.

"We'll have to cross the river on foot," said Thornbury, helping Mneme down again.

The man in black was ahead of them already, clearing a path through the crowd.

"You can't leave that 'ere!" yelled someone behind them, outraged at the coach being abandoned like that.

"Keep it!" the man in black yelled, and kept moving.

There was something very familiar about him. A big man, clearly used to a fight. As he headed down the thick steps to the river below, people steered out of his path like they knew he meant business. She hadn't recognised his voice… but Mneme was beginning to wonder how many details she had missed.

A few steps behind their energetic protector, Mneme and Thornbury looked like any other couple out for a morning's walk on the frozen river. The thought of setting foot on the ice after what had happened last night made Mneme dizzy with fear. Thornbury didn't flinch.

Was he made of bricks?

"Careful as you go," said Thornbury. The charm on

Mneme's boots was holding fast, enabling her to stride across the ice with a semblance of confidence.

It was so infuriating, to be reliant on his everyday magic, having burned all of hers out in that single cry for help. Mneme reached deep inside herself, testing for a spark. There was an ember or two, perhaps. What she needed was rest and time… *not* a hurried jaunt across the Scamander.

A paper bird flew overhead. Mneme might not have noticed it, if she hadn't been glancing around, wondering if any of the glass-blower's creations were still on the loose. This was a smaller, cleverer version of the birds that Mneme had been taught to fold by her mamma.

The first Season that Mneme was Out, before she realised what an impediment her mother was to the process of catching decent husbands, she often returned from a ball or an assembly with dozens of notes from her mamma feathered to the hem of her dress.

Sit up straighter.

Don't talk to that Lady Witting, she's no better than she should be!

Have you heard about the Delvederes?

Why oh why did you have to inherit my red hair?

Take that look off your face, young lady.

This paper bird was thin as a ghost, and fluttered through the air as if tossed by a child. The second Mneme caught sight of it, the paper bird rotated in the air and stared at her.

"Get down!" said Thornbury, and sent a fast fireball to burst the tiny paper bird into sparks and ashes.

Mneme fell behind him. She saw another three paper birds converging on them from various directions, in between the bright huckster tents. A few curious faces turned towards them, but no one was especially fussed. "I suggest we run," she said. "If you want us to get anywhere in particular?"

"That way," said Thornbury, pointing to a narrow avenue of draped stalls selling furs, muffs and fine embroidery.

Mneme darted in that direction, trusting in her charmed boots to stay steady on the ice despite the damp weight of last night's velvet opera dress.

When a ruffian grabbed her from behind, yanking on her hair, her first thought was that she would be helpless without her magic. Her second thought, owing to the childhood training from Mr Zephyr, went directly to her elbow, and hence to her assailant's face.

He shoved her into a stall of trinkets, bringing the owner of the stall over to complain at them both. Mneme kicked out at her attacker and screamed for help — the ordinary way, without disturbing her drowsy, dormant magic.

The trinket merchant started batting both Mneme and her attacker away with a broom. The anti-slip charm on Mneme's boots finally gave way. She slid on the ice, falling hard enough to knock the breath out of her.

Please don't break, she begged the ice.

Her assailant, a flat-faced and heavy-set man she had never seen before, loomed over her for only a moment before he was caught in a chokehold from behind. His eyes rolled up into his head and he fell like a heavy sack of grain on to the ice, revealing the man in black: hood, cloth mask and all.

Mneme blinked.

The bandit scooped her up and kept her moving onward, despite the protests from various stallholders, objecting to the unconscious man who made the place look untidy.

"They'll get you with a littering fine," said Mneme

wildly. So, this was what hysteria felt like. Still, it was better than *are you the Silver Spoon Strangler?* which was the thought uppermost in her head right now. Newspapers were a terrible influence.

The bandit made a small noise that might have been a suppressed laugh, but said nothing more.

Mneme's eyes narrowed. "Where's Mr Thornbury?"

They hurried together around the maze of stalls and attractions. Mneme turned this way and that, following his lead and wondering if the best possible option was run in the opposite direction from where he wanted her to go. "He'll meet us," said the man in black.

"And I'm supposed to trust you?"

He looked pained. As they whirled around a corner Mneme almost had it, the thing that had been bothering her about him from the start. The familiarity.

Henry?

He was the right size and shape to be her cousin, she supposed, though he moved so differently, even held his head in a different way. He moved like a dangerous man, like someone who knew the value of swift and silent. A man who could choke another man until he fell unconscious.

(Again, she thought of the Silver Spoon Strangler, a famous assassin who had struck several wealthy noblemen over the last decade or so, a figure feared almost as much by the gentry as the legendary Ghost of Manticore.)

Was it possible that Henry was capable of something other than being an affable Duke with a billiards obsession? It seemed outlandish. Ridiculous.

Besides, now she was closer… it didn't look like him. At all. The eyebrows were wrong, and the shape of his neck. His eyes were too dark. She was imagining things, clearly. It had been a very difficult couple of days.

They reached a ferry post for rides all the way across

the ice. Without a word, the man in black lifted her physi-
cally into the nearest wheeled boat as if she was his to
protect. No apology, no hesitation. He threw a coin to the
ferryman and bundled in next to Mneme as the horse took
off, dragging the boat onwards.

He felt safe, she realised. Though clearly dangerous to
others. That was why she was reminded of her cousin. No
other reason.

The bandit winced, and shifted on the planking seat
next to her.

"Are you all right?" she asked.

His gloved hand came away dark and wet. "Lightly
stabbed. It will be fine."

"Lightly *stabbed?*"

"Shh, you'll upset the driver," he whispered. "We need
him to get us to the Court bank.

"Upset the driver?"

"They don't like blood on the upholstery."

"We're in a wooden boat," she replied, gasping a little
as they juddered over the ice — clearly the wheels had
been added hastily to this particular rig. "There's no
upholstery."

The bandit gritted his teeth. "But it's so comfortable."

"Are you *hallucinating?*"

"It's possible."

"All across!" called out the ferryman. Their lopsided
boat listed even more to one side as he slowed,
approaching the Court bank of the river. "Sixpence for the
return?"

"No thank you," called out Mneme, bundling her
rescuer out of the boat. He staggered slightly, and she
draped one of his arms over her to support his weight.
"When did you get stabbed?" she whispered furiously at
him, heading for the nearest stone steps leading up off the
river.

To anyone who looked, they might appear to be some drunken couple who'd spent all their coin on gin before lunch time. Wonderful.

"Somewhere between the roof and the river. Got a healing charm for a poor penitent?"

"Not today," she said, though she took a moment to check in on her embers of returning magic, in case they had produced some kind of miracle. "Should we find you a hospice?"

"Healers at the palace."

"We're still heading there?"

"If you want to collect your man. Oh, never mind."

As they came up on to Bridge Street, a covered black stagecoach clattered towards them. Thornbury, a flat cap pulled low on his face, was in the driver's seat. "Let's get going."

The man in black, evidently used to doing things a certain way, lurched towards the stage as if he meant to climb up on the box with the driver.

"You are an idiot," Mneme told him, and gave him a shove into the carriage. She meant to tell Thornbury about the man's injury, but the second she was inside, he took off at a rattling pace.

She settled for producing a clean handkerchief from one of the secret pockets Juno liked to add to every garment she owned, and pressing it hard on the wound in the man in black's stomach.

"Why are people trying to kill us?" she asked, on the off chance that he might be light-headed enough to give her some answers.

He made an amused sort of huffing noise.

Annoyed, she tugged at the black kerchief covering the lower half of his face. "I said…"

There was a warm twang in the air as an illusion charm snapped, and was released. The stranger's face shifted, his eyes bright blue for a moment before the carriage jolted at a bump in the road, and he closed his eyes in pain.

It was Henry after all. Her frivolous, cheerful and utterly harmless dolt of a cousin. Bleeding to death in her arms.

The carriage didn't stop until they reached Wistworia Palace. It must have been only a few minutes — Court simply wasn't that large an island — but it felt like far too long.

"Why didn't you heal him?" Thornbury demanded of Mneme when he saw the state that Henry was in. He leaned over, casting a deep healing charm. Without pausing, he recast the illusion charm also, and tied the kerchief back in place, so that their wounded man no longer looked anything like the Duke of Storm.

Furious and miserable, Mneme removed her blood-soaked gloves and threw them at him. "Because I boiled my magic dry when a certain spellcracker fell into the river last night!" she replied in the chilliest of tones.

Thornbury looked thoroughly startled. "But I took you over the roof."

"Yes. I was very brave about it, *actually*. When do I get to ask my questions? I've been saving them up."

He gazed at her helplessly.

A palace footman approached, snapping to attention in

response to a single word spoken by Mr Thornbury: "*Perse-verance.*"

Everything rolled forth rather quickly after that, and nothing about the bustling efficiency of the palace emergency protocol was conducive to further conversation.

~

BEING a member of the Seabourne family meant a great many more invitations to events at the palace than one could possibly accept. As far as Mneme was concerned, even a few were far too many.

She had been to Wistworia Palace as a child more than once, as part of her mother's retinue. On one occasion, she and Metis and Henry were garbed in identical silk sailor suit outfits at the behest of her late aunt, the Duchess of Storm.

Miss Mnemosyne Seabourne was invited to Wistworia in her own right (not merely as an adjunct to her mamma) six years or so ago, for her presentation to the Old Queen upon coming Out in Society, and again three months later, for the funeral of the Old Queen, and subsequent coronation of Young Queen Aud.

It made for an awkward first Season, juggling mourning blacks and lilacs with tea parties and half the usual number of balls.

Mneme only knew a few areas of the palace with any familiarity: the reception gardens, the grand crystal hall, and the debutante gallery. Today, she was hurried into a gaping parlour hung with heavy curtains.

There were so many portraits hung so close together in their giant gilded frames that there was no need for wallpaper. It was like being glared at by a kaleidoscope of postage stamps featuring someone else's grumpiest uncles.

There was a full tea service, piping hot. Porcelain cups with a pattern of cornflowers and poppies.

She was alone.

For the first time in her living memory, Mneme did not fancy a cup of tea. She couldn't even bring herself to sit down.

She watched the clock tick on the mantlepiece, for more than half an hour. She was exhausted and ragged, with Henry's blood on her borrowed opera gown, and boots that were starting to feel wet on the inside as well as out.

Finally the door swung open, and Mr Thornbury entered. He had changed his clothes, she noted sourly. Fully buttoned up, with a new cravat. If he had taken the time to bathe before he came to find her, she was going to crack that teapot over his head.

"Are you hurt?" he asked, looking her over carefully.

"It's not my blood."

At the sharp tone in her voice, he relaxed, as if Mneme being angry at him was a sure sign she was perfectly all right. (Hadn't he learned yet that ladies could do and feel more than one thing at a time?)

"Henry's healing fine," he informed her. "The palace physician is finishing up with him shortly."

"So, you can answer some questions?"

Thornbury sagged, as if he had expected this. "Yes. We have time now." He reached for her hands as if to clasp them both in his.

She pulled away and sat stiffly on the ridiculously pretty couch, not even caring if she got blood all over it. The palace cleaning staff were probably bursting with spells for that sort of thing. "Who is Henry?"

Thornbury sat opposite her. After a brief moment of awkwardness when she failed to pour the tea despite his evident expectation, he reached for the pot himself and poured two cups. "He's your cousin, the Duke of Storm."

"Don't toy with me."

"Some of the answers to your questions will be secrets I am not allowed to tell," Thornbury warned her. "But given the events of today, there's a little more flexibility than might otherwise be the case. Henry is an agent of the Crown. So am I."

Mneme wasn't entirely sure what that meant. She said nothing, and did not touch the cup of tea he poured for her. Somehow, that unsettled Thornbury enough to keep talking — a good trick she must remember in future.

He took a deep breath before he began, and swallowed nearly half of his tea in one gulp. "Do you remember asking me if I would take the Seabourne name when we married?"

"Of course," Mneme said stiffly.

"That was an easy decision, because Thornbury isn't a family name. My father chose it for me to make sure we were never publicly connected."

"And your father is?

"Octavian Swift, Queen's Consultant." He said it as if it was the heaviest, most tragic secret he had ever shared with anyone.

"I've never heard of him," said Mneme.

"Few have. On paper, he's the dullest of Her Majesty's advisors, all paperwork and filing. In truth, he's the Queen's spymaster. He runs secret agents around the Teacup Isles and the Continent, collecting information to keep the country safe."

"And you're one of these agents," Mneme said quietly. "You and Henry — all that travel you do, all those back and forth capers of the Duke of Storm. The parties and the social whirl. You were doing that in public, and at the same time…"

"Everyone knows Henry is the Queen's man," said Mr Thornbury. "It's the traditional role of the Duke of Storm when the monarch is unmarried. He speaks on her behalf, hosts parties for foreign visitors, that sort of thing. It's a remarkably good cover for his other job, especially as most people assume he's a nitwit. He's not even pretending that part," he added. "Being ridiculously cheerful and blurting out random nonsense is all him. He just… has a lot more going on under the surface than most people."

"You said his other job, but you mean *your* other job," she corrected, holding his gaze steadily. "*Both* of you are agents of the Crown."

"Yes." He admitted it so easily, as if he had not turned her entire world upside down.

"You told me I would be a scholar's wife!" It came out more plaintive than Mneme might have wished. She wanted so badly to be strong right now. Strong, and graceful and quietly furious. She had the furious part down, at least.

Thornbury winced. "I know I did."

"Perhaps you should tell me whom I would really be marrying? Because the life you described to me, of occasional spellcracking interspersed with library research and happy domesticity, does not really match with the life of a Queen's agent, or the son of a spymaster, or whatever you are."

She wanted to cry. She would hate herself if she started crying right now.

Mr Thornbury hesitated. "I was not dishonest about the life I thought we would lead together, Mneme. All this — I was supposed to be done with it by now. That was decided before I even met you. Henry chose to settle down, to start taking his title seriously and try to father a son. Hijinks and secret messages and stabbings on rooftops are for men with fewer personal responsibilities. Finding him a wife who wouldn't turn out to be an enemy agent was my last official task for the Crown. Our retirement was made official *months* ago."

Mneme's mind was all a whirl. "Does Juno know all this?"

"He told her about his past on their wedding night. As I intended to with you…"

She could tell from the hopeful look on his face that Thornbury thought this was a reasonable plan.

"*After* we were bound in matrimony," she noted sharply. "After our fates were inextricably tied to those of our husbands."

"I know it's not fair," he conceded. "I didn't expect to find you. To have someone like you in my life. And when I realised what we could have together — I was so relieved that my old career was behind me. That I didn't have to make a choice."

It didn't feel like it was behind either of them right now. She still had Henry's blood on her gown.

"You can't turn it off, can you?" Mneme accused. "If you see something that endangers the Crown, you will act. Like you did last night: investigating the printer's tent, finding Sevinny's body. That wasn't for my benefit, it was because you noticed something out of place. If you come across something dangerous in future, you won't just leave it to the other agents of the Crown. You will act."

He hesitated, and she saw a world of excuses in his eyes. He was trying to think of the right words to convince her that this was a single, one-off occurrence. That being a spymaster's son was something you could actually retire from.

If he lied now, she could never trust him.

"Yes," said Thornbury admitted heavily. "I will always act. Always."

Mneme understood him better now. She wasn't happy

about it, but at least she had more information. If he had waited until their wedding night… how could Juno have possibly forgiven her own husband for this?

"Tell me about Sevinny," she said after a moment. "Did you kill him?"

Mr Thornbury choked on the dregs of his tea. "Gods, no. Is that what you think of me?"

"We have established I don't know as much about you as I imagined," Mneme snapped. "You draw the line at assassination?"

"It's not one of my special skills."

"How comforting."

"You should drink the tea," he blurted out, putting down his empty cup. "Vervain and lemon-grass. It will help you recover your magic."

"Thank you," said Mneme, her voice still sharp with anger. "That was very thoughtful." She raised the cup — no longer hot — to her lips and drank in small vicious sips. It did make her feel better. Somehow, that was the most infuriating thing of all. "So. Who killed him?"

"I don't know yet. But I intend to find out."

"Did it have something to do with my pamphlets?" Her voice gave way a little. The business with the sordid cartoon of the Queen was bad enough, but she did not know how to process the idea that her portal campaign might have caused a man's death.

"Not exactly," said Thornbury. "It was bad luck that you chose that particular printer. I didn't know myself about the connexion until after you reported seeing Sevinny there, the day of the first snow."

"But if he commissioned that awful print, and was killed in the printer's tent…"

"Sevinny did not commission the print, nor release it. I don't think he had anything to do with the theft of your pamphlets, either."

Mneme blinked. "He didn't commission the print? But he said…"

"Sevinny was good at saying things, my dear. He filled the air with words, to distract people from suspecting his true purpose. That was his special skill. Perhaps he had satirical prints on the brain at the time? The truth is, Fenchurch the printer was Sevinny's informant. While it's possible that Fenchurch killed Sevinny and went to ground, it's far more likely that Fenchurch has been abducted by the people responsible for Sevinny's death."

"I'm missing something," said Mneme, interested despite herself. "Why don't you think Sevinny was the one behind the print?"

"Because," said Thornbury. "He was my colleague, another agent of the Crown."

"But he was an anti-royalist!" she protested. "Quite the loudest anti-royalist in the city, according to Juno!"

"Yes," said Thornbury. "The best part was that he meant every word of it. Hated the very idea of monarchy. That didn't stop him being loyal to the Queen. It's rather useful, to have agents in enemy camps. My father has made a specialty of placing his people in the most unexpected positions — and of turning those in unexpected positions over to our side. I'm not sure which way around it was with Sevinny. But he was the Queen's man, and he died in her service."

He said it matter-of-factly, as if this was the normal way of things.

Mneme nodded, her mouth becoming thin. "And now his wife is a widow," she said, very quietly.

This was a fact that Mr Thornbury could not refute.

ALL WIVES TOGETHER

Mneme did not know how to silence all the whirling thoughts in her head. She had been so sure of Mr Thornbury as a man worthy of her trust. A man who desired an equal partner in marriage.

Now, with these secrets revealed, she felt unmoored. As if she had been set floating on the Lyric Sea in a swan-shaped boat.

She needed time to think, away from him. After a few minutes of awkward tea drinking, she got that chance. One of the royal footmen knocked discreetly on the door to call him away.

Mr Thornbury hesitated before leaving Mneme. "Needless to say…"

"I won't breathe a word of your secrets. Juno knows everything, though?" She would have one friend she could confide in, at least. As soon as she knew what it was she wanted to confide.

"She knows about *Henry*," admitted Thornbury reluctantly.

Ridiculous man. "And you think she hasn't worked out

that his private spellcracker must be involved in all aspects of his work?"

"I know she was not informed about my family connexions."

No one to confide in fully, then. Mneme was quite alone.

"I'll take it to my grave," she sighed. "Off you go, then. Work to do. Don't mind me."

Before Mr Thornbury could take his leave, a boisterous Henry burst into the portrait parlour. "I say, what's with the lollygagging? We have a lead on where those black-guards are holding Fenchurch!" He broke off as he saw Mneme. "Ah."

"Masterful secret agent you have here," Mneme said dryly. "I feel very safe."

"Mnemo!" Henry pounced on her for a warm embrace. He seemed thoroughly fit and not in the least stabbed. He had even found time for a bath, which Mneme resented deeply. "Topping rescue. In both directions. You know the whole of it, now?"

"Apparently so." She watched Mr Thornbury's face to see if he also thought she had been told *the whole of it*. He was, as ever, difficult to read.

"That'll save time. Excellent news for Juno, she's been fierce to tell you for months now. Simply batty about it. Are you off home? Tell a footman to wrangle you up a sleigh if you like. Best pack you safely off to Storm Bolt as soon as possible."

The thought of heading out into the snow again, across the frozen river, made Mneme shudder. "Any chance I could visit the palace baths to tidy up first?"

For the first time, Henry took in the state of her. "Gad, yes. Not a worry. Best baths in the city, this palace. They go on for miles. Off you pop, we'll be back before you know it."

"Really," Mr Thornbury said with weight to his words. "Don't worry."

Easier said than done.

~

HENRY WAS NOT wrong about the baths. The Old Queen was famously cuckoo for bathing rituals, and had installed a grand Pump Room along with several glossy marble pools and fountains beneath Wistworia Palace.

Mneme had been down here once before, on the eve of her debutante presentation. Clusters of girls in muslin shifts, bobbing about in the pool and gossiping about hairstyles and gloves. Mneme had spent most of her time wishing she had a good book, as she ran out of everything she had to say about hairstyles and gloves in the first few minutes.

She was better at being friends with women now, in comparison to her sulky younger self. Still, she could not quite embrace the notion of public bathing. Too many flashbacks to the Isle of Bath, where the aristocratic mammas engaged in savage and ruthless matchmaking rituals.

Mneme heard a horror story once about a seventeen-year-old Earl's fourth daughter whose mamma locked her in a bathing machine with a handsome foreign Marquise in order to see her compromised and wed in short order. It turned out the Marquise in question had no interest in the young lady, being happily wed to another handsome gentleman — the girl promptly took her opportunity and ran off to become an opera singer while she had the chance. Still, one lady's happy ending was another lady's tragedy.

Today, the palace baths were empty. It was a strange thing to stroll through the domed halls of echoes and temperate pools. Mneme, wearing the thin flannel shift provided to her by a helpful maid, tested each bath in turn to find the right temperature.

Being alone was a luxury she rarely got to experience.

Several pools along, she found the perfect balance of heat and promptly removed her shift, sliding with a sigh into the warm water. The palace baths were heated by magic — an entirely decadent use of charmed tile all year around — and yet she could smell a whiff of sulphur somewhere, probably added for authenticity.

She had three blissful minutes of solitude before interruption.

A child screamed somewhere, and another giggled loudly. There was the pattering of feet, and a splashing sound.

"Wash your feet before you get in the shared pool, Raoul," said a weary female voice. "Out of there, you little whelk. I want you to watch the baby."

A tiny boy, still dry, lurched past the pool where Mneme was ensconced. He was buck naked, his hair sticking up wildly. Against all the odds for such a small child, he was already perfectly clean. He stared at her. "Who are you?"

"Hello," said Mneme, dipping deeper under the water. "Have we met?"

A woman in a borrowed palace robe stepped into view. She held a baby in one arm, and held a slightly older boy, wet as a fish from the market, by the other. She looked at Mneme with a sort of weary politeness that Mneme recognised as 'oh gods, I thought I wouldn't have to talk to people.' Then, recognition dawned.

"Oh," said Mrs Fenchurch, the printer's wife. "It's you."

THEY ORDERED tea to the Tadpole Room, a shallow children's pool that allowed for as much safe splashing as the two little boys desired. The baby, after showing mild fascination with the water, eventually fell asleep in a basket and was discreetly nudged under the table.

Mneme, also in a soft palace robe, poured the tea and passed the sandwiches.

"They gave me a nursemaid," Mrs Fenchurch blurted out, then looked around guiltily. "They asked if I needed more than one! Can you believe it?"

Privately, Mneme thought that all mothers probably needed more than one, but she understood how strange it must be to be here, as a guest of Her Majesty. "I imagine you'd rather have your husband back."

"Exactly," said Mrs Fenchurch, looking relieved. "I know it's ungrateful of me, but all this… rooms in the palace, servants. It's like walking around a museum half the time. I'm terrified this lot will break something — or I will. I wanted to go to my sister's place at the seaside, but they…" She glanced warily over at her sons, who were blowing bubbles in the water. "Those fellows reckon we're not safe."

It was warm here, with the steam of all the pools pressing around them. The tea was refreshing. Mneme bit into a cake. "Why are you not safe?"

"I'm a witness," Mrs Fenchurch said, in a whisper. "I saw what happened to that Mr Sevinny. At least, I think I saw. The Queen's man, he said I might be in danger, that enemies of the Crown might snatch my boys to make my husband talk."

Mneme could not imagine how terrifying that might be. "Did you know your husband was — helping the Crown with their inquiries?"

Mrs Fenchurch rolled her eyes. "He was a snitch, you mean? I knew. He's been in that Sevinny's pocket for years now, letting him know who's ordering what. It's amazing what people will tell a printer when they're negotiating for a cheap rate. Any man who wants to spread sedition against the Crown has to start by knocking off an order of hand-bills. And you'd be amazed how many traitors and troublemakers feel the need to put their words down in a manifesto. One time, they nabbed this crime boss because he made the mistake of paying for his brother's gothic novels to be published. I never liked the risk or the danger, but spying for the Crown has brought in a fair bit of gingerbread for our lot over the years. How else could we have afforded a spanking new printing press?"

Mneme caught her breath, wondering if anyone had informed Mrs Fenchurch of what had happened to her press.

The printer's wife gave her another of those weary looks. "Oh aye, I know. Some muckers hexed her to send Sevinny's body into the drink, and almost took the Queen's man with him. He told me earlier. I threw a plate at him."

Thornbury had visited Mrs Fenchurch before he came to see Mneme? But of course he had. Work before personal.

"You must be very worried," Mneme offered.

"All them takings we hoped for from the Frost Fair come to nothing, and now our livelihood's gone through the ice," muttered the woman. "And here I am, sitting in a palace like Lady Muck with hot and cold running nurse-maids, and chocolate after every meal. The second it's all over, we'll be back to the old grind, copying letters for pennies." She sighed. "You mean my husband, I suppose. Aye, I'm worried about him, too."

A shy nursemaid came along with a footman to assist. Mrs Fenchurch allowed them to gather the children and take them off to the nursery, with only a hint of reluctance.

"Better enjoy it while I can," she said in an undertone to Mneme.

With the children out of the way, both women went to an outer chamber to garb themselves in fresh day clothes that had been put out for them — carefully chosen day dresses with warm pelisses to lay over the top. They could not be the Queen's hand-me-downs, but was it normal to provide clothing for guests?

Mneme had never visited anywhere without her own wardrobe, despite Juno's insistence on lending her clothes at every opportunity; perhaps she, like Mrs Fenchurch, was officially a charity case now.

"Best not to ask where it all comes from," said Mrs Fenchurch with a roll of her eyes. "I'll be the one breaking our Raoul's heart when I tell him he won't be going home with them three feathered caps he's collected since we got here."

As they left the thick warmth of the bathing hall to the chillier upper rooms of the palace, more footmen appeared to steer them along a corridor, apparently with purpose. They were ushered into a small parlour featuring shelves of colour co-ordinated books (bound only in blue and cream), and matching curtains. The chairs were made of some kind of wicker basketry.

Mrs Ceto Sevinny, in a sprigged muslin day dress and floral bonnet, was waiting for them at a table covered in cakes. "Oh look," she said without a hint of humour. "It's the Spy Widows Club."

"*Our* men are still alive," said Mrs Fenchurch in an acid tone worthy of a Dowager. "Despite your husband's best efforts, madam." She sat down, and put a wedge of cherry cake in her mouth.

Mneme did not want to be here, but she could not miss this opportunity to learn more. She sat, and helped herself to a scone. "I'm sorry for your loss, Mrs Sevinny," she said politely.

"No widow's weeds in the palace loaner wardrobe?" sniped Mrs Fenchurch.

"They're on order from Ambrodes," said Mrs Sevinny haughtily. "I wouldn't wear clothes that belong to other people."

There was no answer for that. Mneme scooped jam and cream on to her scone.

Thornbury and Henry might be anywhere right now. Sliding over rooftops, battling ruffians, hurling hexes and enacting a daring rescue attempt.

And here she was. With the wives, the tea and the cake. This was the future she could look forward to. Waiting to find out if she, too, should put in an order of black taffeta garments to Ambrodes, the most exclusive department store in Town.

If her magic returned properly, at least she could transform her old clothes to black so as not to waste the money.

"You're engaged to him, aren't you?" Mrs Sevinny broke in, her eyes glittering as she regarded Mneme. "The Queen's man. Agent Thornbury."

"I'm sure you shouldn't call him that in public," Mneme said primly. She was not sure if she was currently engaged. She had a lot of thinking to do, and she did not wish to discuss it with strangers.

"This isn't public," said Mrs Sevinny, breaking an iced bun into several smaller pieces. "All wives together. You, at least, have a chance to get out before the life eats you up."

"The life?" Mneme repeated.

Mrs Fenchurch reached for another slice of the cherry cake and munched on it. "The life of being married to men who put the Queen before everything else," she agreed.

The two women looked at each other with an angry sort of sympathy.

"You'd better watch him," Mrs Sevinny added to Mneme. "That man of yours. Cold as ice."

Mneme was startled. She had never thought of Thornbury that way.

"Better that than my Fenchurch," Mrs Fenchurch said. "Too soft-hearted for his own good. No more sense than he was born with." Her hand trembled, setting her cake fork rattling against the plate.

"They'll bring him back alive," Mneme said quietly.

Mrs Fenchurch gave her a bleak look. "Will they, now?"

"Oh, this is where you all are!" Two new ladies entered the parlour, decked out in what could only be described as full Frost Fair finery. It was the Countess of Balmady and Mrs Threnod.

The elderly Countess had only made a discreet nod towards the current fashion with her choice of jewels on the night of the book club. Today, she embraced it entirely. Her scooped pelisse was silver velvet with silver snowflake buttons over layers of ivory silk. She wore diamond earrings that looked like bursts of falling snow on tiny wires and a matching spiked brooch. Her bonnet looked like a winter forest had exploded on it, so weighed down was it with white ribbons and fronds of fresh pine tree. Every edge of sleeve, collar or hem was trimmed with blinding white fur.

Mrs Threnod, beside her, wore almost exactly the same outfit in a dove grey, and pearls wherever the Countess wore diamonds. They looked like a holiday card of two enchantresses who had been decorated for the season by a horde of small children.

Mrs Fenchurch stared at the newcomers as if she expected Mr Punch and his puppet pals to burst out from one of the dresses. Mrs Sevinny was equally startled.

"We've called for fresh tea," said the Countess of Balmady, and sat down without being asked. Mrs Threnod hovered for a moment, then sat opposite her, in the only spare seat. "How are you, my dear?"

Mrs Sevinny blinked. "Are you talking to me?"

"Of course," said the Countess.

"Of course," echoed Mrs Threnod.

"My deepest condolences on the loss of your husband."

"Condolence," added Mrs Threnod. There was a brief pause, in which the Countess gave her companion a pointed look, as if she expected her to say something more. "And how very unusual to find the wife of an anti-royalist sheltering here in the palace. Truly ours is a gracious queen."

"Indeed," said the Countess with a definite nod. "Well said, my dear."

This was the most bewildering double act. Was Mneme witnessing a meeting of the Secret Senate, or some kind of nervous breakdown?

"I'm not *sheltering* here," Mrs Sevinny said, her voice rising in fury. "I wouldn't accept the Queen's patronage if she presented it on a tea trolley."

Fresh tea arrived on, indeed, a trolley. All five women sat, straight-backed, as two extremely handsome palace footmen arranged the new pot and cups, along with a whole new range of cakes.

Mrs Fenchurch looked worn at the edges by this inter-ruption of genteel, over-dressed ladies. Mneme saw any further opportunity to question her about the Sevinny affair slipping away through her fingers.

Mrs Threnod waved the footmen away, and poured the tea herself in a ritual that was almost mesmerising to watch. She set the cups out an equal distance from each other, clipped exactly half a sugar cube and one and half slices of lemon into each (using pearl-handled clippers from her own handbag), and poured with the precision of an alchemist.

No milk was offered, or served. Each cup received three sharp stirs and was set in front of the recipient: first the Countess, then Mrs Sevinny, then Mrs Fenchurch, then Mneme.

(Mneme wondered only for a moment why she was graced with the last cup only to realise that of course, the other ladies were all married, putting her at the bottom of a pecking order of sorts.)

Mrs Threnod put the clippers back into her bag and then served herself tea, to which she added no sugar and no lemon. "Where were we?" she asked, looking around. "Ah, Mrs Sevinny was mocking our intelligence by claiming to be some sort of revolutionary."

"What?" demanded Mrs Sevinny, quite out of sorts. "I tell you…"

"Come dear, we know the truth," sighed the Countess. "You're as much of a royalist as all of us, your late husband doubly so. Long live the Queen," she added with a sip and a smile.

Mrs Sevinny stopped arguing, but drank her tea with frustrated fury.

Mrs Fenchurch poured her own tea into the saucer to cool it, and then dipped a shortbread in. No one even winced. The Countess and Mrs Threnod were too busy staring at Mrs Sevinny, as if trying to drag her secrets out by the power of judgy thoughts.

Mneme raised her own cup to her lips, but did not drink. She hated tea without milk. Lemon and sugar was insult on top of injury.

She could feel her magic returning with painful slowness, a quiet hum beneath her skin. If she didn't have that to worry about, then her all of her thoughts would be entirely caught up with Thornbury and Henry, fretting about whatever dangerous shenanigans they were up to out there.

Something shifted the mood in the tea parlour. The tension between the five women eased a little. The right cup of tea could mend bridges and move mountains. This was not the right cup of tea, but it was the thought that counted.

Mrs Fenchurch slumped in her chair, the exhaustion of the week finally catching up with her. Mrs Sevinny shivered in her sprigged muslin, which was more appropriate for summer picnics than winter tea parties in palaces. She leaned her chin against her hand. The Countess of Balmady began to snore. Even the ever-taut Mrs Threnod was deathly still.

Mneme had not drunk the tea. Had anyone noticed? She sighed back against the fairly uncomfortable wicker chair, letting her head tilt back and her eyes fall mostly closed. Through the flicker of her lashes, she waited to see what happened next.

The Countess snored again, an ungainly snort that could not be faked; no lady would ever let such a noise out of her mouth deliberately.

Mrs Sevinny's bonnet fell entirely off, tumbling to the floor.

Mrs Threnod rose to her feet, straight-backed and sharp as a tack.

She didn't put sugar or lemon in her own tea, Mneme thought to herself, remembering those pearl-handled tongs. Had the others been poisoned? Enchanted?

Mrs Threnod moved behind Mrs Fenchurch, and removed something from her purse: a long, white silken cord. With the same precision that she had employed in the pouring of tea, the Countess's companion wrapped the cord around Mrs Fenchurch's throat.

Mneme had nothing to work with but what came immediately to hand — a full cup of tea, a cake plate, and what few threads of magic had crept to her, like a new brook trickling out of the side of a mountain. Her magic would not, could not be enough.

But that teapot was close, and piping hot.

Before Mrs Threnod could tighten the cord, Mneme lunged for the teapot and hurled it directly into her face.

TWO CONVERSATIONS IN WISTWORIA PALACE

The Queen of the Teacup Isles was exceptionally pretty, and not only because she wore tiaras and lived in a palace. She had a round face, light brown skin, the sweetest smile in the world, and spiralling black curls of hair that were always pinned up in some clever way. Today it was a series of bronze hair clips displaying frogs and dragonflies.

The Queen of the Teacup Isles did not bother with fashion, as it bothered her enough for the both of them. There was not a single snowflake anywhere on her attire.

She was twenty three years old, the same age as Mneme. She had been Queen for six years.

Queen Aud did not order tea, but a proper luncheon spread including glasses of ratafia, small chicken pies, and an excellent salad of beets.

Mneme would have rather liked to eat some of it, but she was too busy retelling her story (which had lacked suffi-cient detail the first time around) to grab more than a dainty mouthful or two, in between the Queen's questions.

"My favourite part," said the Queen with a happy sigh.

"Is where the Duke of Storm and your Mr Thornbury came rushing in to save you all, and found you had not only caught the infamous Silver Spoon Strangler for them, but had tied her up with the curtain cords. What an adventurous life you lead, Miss Seabourne."

"Not usually," said Mneme. "I'm a dull sort of thing mostly. Bookworm and wallflower, rolled into one."

"So you *say*," the Queen said, not believing a word of it. She shook her head amiably. "I never liked that Mrs Threnod. When the Countess of Balmady used to come to tea with my mother, she always brought that frightful old witch with her. Once, she caught me adding a second sugar cube to my tea and she rapped me across the knuckles with a spoon!"

"I know what you mean," said Mneme. "Still, there are so many horrible old ladies among the gentry. How were we to know one was genuinely an assassin?"

"And a filthy traitor too," the Queen added, her tone quite grim. "Murdering my agents with one hand, and publishing vicious cartoons about me with the other. All because that hideous Duke of Glass is convinced that if I die without an heir, the Court of Lords will finally let him be King. Cousins are dreadful, Miss Seabourne, I recommend you never have any. Oh, that reminds me!" She leapt up from the table with a great deal of bounce, and ran to the sideboard where a large brown paper parcel was waiting, tied up with string.

"Is that for me?" Mneme asked, wondering what on earth the Queen might have chosen as a gift for her.

"It's your pamphlets, silly. I'm returning them to you. Though you might want to reprint them, I picked out a couple of spelling errors on the one I read and, well after that I went simply wild with the red pen. But I enjoyed it very much." She smiled that beautiful smile of hers, all warmth and joy. The smile that had held their kingdom together, against all enemies.

"You have my pamphlets," Mneme repeated, not sure she was hearing right.

"Of course. I take great interest in matters that affect public opinion, and once I learned that public opinion was shifting in the matter of portal travel for women, I was all for it. Why do you think they picked that cartoon in particular, to ridicule the idea that the Queen of their country might be in favour of equality between the sexes?"

Mneme was still stuck on the part where the Queen of the Teacup Isles had been in possession of her pamphlets all this time. "Did you seize them from Mrs Threnod?"

"Oh no," said the Queen in all innocence. "I stole them in the first place, I'm afraid. Sevinny tipped me off about them, and I sent my maid Baines to snaffle them from the printers. They're all there, except for a handful we leaked deliberately to the Secret Senate. I knew those old biddies had been dragging their feet on portal travel, and there were rumours they wanted to squash your campaign. I wanted to shake them up a bit. Also I wanted to read the thing, to find out whose side you were on."

"Whose side?"

"You know," the Queen said, her dark eyes holding Mneme intensely. "To find out if you were one of those dreadful ladies who thinks only married women are deserving of rights and privileges. *I'm* not married, and while I might be finally convinced to hitch myself to some foreign prince or dashing naval captain if it means I never have to step into a swan-shaped boat again… well. I shouldn't have to make that choice. Should I?"

"So, what do you think now?" Mneme asked. "Are we on the same side?"

The Queen's face broke out into pure joy again. The

smile that launched a thousand portals. "I rather think we are, Miss Seabourne."

~

As IT TURNED OUT, it really did just take one conversation with the Queen to change the world. Mneme couldn't wait to tell Juno — though of course, the Duchess of Storm would never admit she had been wrong about something. She'd probably find some way to turn it all into an 'I told you so.'

(And of course, Juno wasn't entirely wrong… the Queen was absolutely led by public opinion as much as her own convenience.)

Still, they had won.

Mneme needed to talk to Mr Thornbury. They hadn't had much of a chance in all the chaos after she took out Mrs Threnod with a teapot to the face.

Henry was little help in the aftermath. He just kept laughing about the whole affair. Even when an alchemist had to be called, to provide the antidote for whatever strange sleeping potion Mrs Threnod had used to dose the other ladies.

Mneme rather thought Mr Thornbury had tried to draw her aside at one point, but Henry was hanging off him, and so they barely managed to exchange a word or two before she was summoned away to wait upon the Queen.

She was so caught up in her thoughts now that she found herself wandering in quite the wrong part of the palace. Just as she was about to give up and pull one of the bell ribbons to ask for help, an unassuming man in black popped out of a library at her. "Can I help you, miss?"

"I, uh," Mneme faltered. "Does Mr Thornbury have an office around here, do you know?" If he worked for the

Crown, even secretly, surely he at least had a cubby or something where he could sit with a cup of tea and bounce hexes off the ceiling while pondering whatever grand kingdom-threatening secrets he had gathered.

The man stared at her, and disappeared back in to the library. A moment later, a grey-haired man who must be a senior librarian emerged in his place. This one had the confidence of an ageing under-butler, though his clothes were faded and dusty. "Let me show you the way, miss," he said, and set off down another corridor.

A palace was as bad as a city for getting lost in. At least the ground underfoot was heated stone and not frozen river water.

The under-butler, or over-librarian, led her to a large room filled with desks, papers and empty cups.

"Is no one allowed to dust in here?" Mneme asked in surprise.

"No, miss. All very top secret stuff in here." The man leaned against a desk. "Thornbury, was it you said you wanted? He's not in here much."

"Well, he's a very busy man." Her eyes narrowed. "You needn't keep up the pretence. I know who you are."

"Do you indeed, miss?" His stance changed, slightly. He went from an illusion of unimportance to commanding a room.

"You have a very distinctive nose," she said wistfully. "And a way of blending in when you don't want to be noticed. It seems impossible to believe that changing your son's name was enough to ensure no one knew the connexion. Mr Swift," she added, politely.

Octavian Swift, the Queen's... consultant? Well, whatever his dull job description actually was hardly mattered. He was the Queen's spymaster.

He nodded his head now with equal politeness. "Miss

Seabourne. I'm told you're very quick at putting things together."

"Did he tell you that with an air of exasperation?"

Mr Swift's mouth twisted a little, another very familiar expression on this calm older gentleman's face. "He may have done. Congratulations on closing the case of the Silver Spoon Strangler. It's a matter of great personal embarrassment that I don't already have you on my payroll."

"That's very sweet," said Mneme. "But my mother despairs of my life choices. If I should go so far as to earn a salary, she might die of the vapours."

"It wasn't an offer."

"And yet here I am, turning it down." She had the sensation of being under close observation, which was bad enough at balls when it was done by dowagers. Alone in a room in a palace with the father of a man she had rather hoped to marry at some point, it was entirely unpleasant. "May I ask you a question, Mr Swift?"

The spymaster gave her the politest of nods. "Apparently my agent saw fit to tell you a great deal about our work. Therefore, I am an open book."

That wasn't in the least true, and she could see that he no more believed it than she did. "How did you feel when your son told you he was stepping away from this business of yours?"

Octavian Swift blinked. "I did not believe he intended to follow through with that particular plan. I still don't."

There it was, the reason that Mneme felt like she was the enemy, for all his politeness. "Is that why he keeps finding himself in the midst of vital missions, despite his retirement?"

"Retirement," the spymaster scoffed. "It's all very well for wealthy fribbles like your Duke Henry to play at spycraft for a year or two, and then give it up for wives and babies. But for men like me — men like Charles — the work is never done."

Charles. She had never called Thornbury by his first name. She got the impression he didn't like it, or didn't connect it with himself. Perhaps, as a wife, she might use it in private. Perhaps not. Her mamma would call her papa Mr Seabourne until the day she died, and Mneme knew other wives who happily used their husband's last name, or a nickname.

"What if he wants something else?" she tried.

Mr Swift gave her an impatient look. "Have you met him? The man is only alive when he's hunting the answer to a question."

That was true, she must concede.

"Take this matter," Swift went on. "We never assigned Agent Thornbury to investigate the Silver Spoon Strangler, or to dig into the machinations of the Duke of Glass. He found the threads on his own, brought them to us. *After* his so-called retirement. When he and Storm got the lead about Fenchurch, they didn't pass it to another operative. They ran off themselves, rescued the damned printer, brought him home to his wife and kids. Now the villainous Duke of Glass has had his treason plot uncovered, and he's disappeared somewhere on the Continent, drat his eyes. I need to send someone to find him. Who should I send?"

Mneme's heart sank. "You should send your best," she said.

"Indeed I should."

"How do you see this ending?" she asked after a moment's thought. "You give your son the most dangerous of missions, or he takes them himself. Over and over. Is there any resolution where he does not die in action?"

Octavian Swift gave her a canny look. "Someday, when he's battered and cynical enough to do it, he'll retire to my desk. He'll make the hard decisions about who goes out into the field. And he'll be brilliant at it."

"If he lives long enough to get there," muttered Mneme.

"Oh yes," said the father of the man she loved. "If he doesn't, well. He wasn't the man for the job."

PORTALS FOR LADIES

After her unpleasant conversation with Octavian Swift, Mneme left the palace. She did not stop to check on her other acquaintances in residence: Mrs Fenchurch would be distracted now that she had her husband back and a life to rebuild. Mrs Sevinny would be just as busy dealing with the fact that her own husband was gone forever.

Mneme was officially a friend of the Queen now, so maids happily loaded her up with everything she needed including new buttoned boots and a fur-trimmed hood with warming charms installed. She still did not trust that she could provide her own warmth, though her magic was healing nicely.

A sleigh was provided, but Mneme decided to walk. Even if that meant, once she reached the river, crossing the Frost Fair one more time.

The great frost was predicted to last several more weeks, and various shops and entertainments had thoroughly established themselves in their temporary home. Mneme noticed familiar corners and avenues from her previous visits, making this no different to the Arcade of

Ladylike Dainties, or one of Juno's other favourite haunts.

Juno. Mneme missed her fiercely. Almost as much as she missed the quietness and solitude of the Seabourne estate on the Isle of Memory. Home. Storm Bolt would never be home, though it was a pleasanter place to live this winter than it had ever been before. She belonged to it now, as Juno's friend, in a way she never had when she was merely the old Duchess' niece.

Trudging over the ice, her eye constantly distracted by the various stalls and performances, Mneme found herself heading for the street of stalls that had once housed Fenchurch and Sons. The printer's tent was gone, of course, under the ice. But someone had sealed it all over good as new, and the glass-blower had taken the opportunity to expand.

Where his stall had previously featured clever jewellery, baubles and drinking cups, now there were gilded cages, straw baskets, and a long table of artificial grass. There was also quite a crowd gathered around, cooing and awwing at what they saw.

Mneme waited her turn, and pushed forward to see for herself.

The glass-blower had an entire stall of live glass hedgehogs. The size of teacups, they stumbled around adorably and peered at their audience. Many had ribbons tied around them.

"The must-have courting gift of the year," announced the glass-blower. He caught sight of Mneme's surprised face, and tipped his hat to her. "What started with an unexpected bit of magic has worked out rather nicely for me," he said in her general direction. "Especially once the little critters started having babies." He went back to his patter for the crowd.

So, one thing less to feel guilty about.

~

MNEME RETURNED to Storm Bolt later in the day, carefully cradling a warm straw basket containing the sweetest glass hedgehog that ever drew breath. Mr Thornbury came down the stairs, rushing to meet her.

"They told me you'd left the palace," he said, doing that thing that she had realised now he always did after a time apart — checking her over to be sure that she was unharmed. It might be annoying if another man did that, but this one had reason to be concerned for her safety. She would allow it.

After all, seeing him still gave her a quick jolt of fear and relief all at once, as she remembered he had fallen through the ice, and barely survived.

"I wanted a walk," said Mneme, taking a step backwards. "And to come home. I can only be waited on hand and foot in a strange place for so long before I start feeling like a burglar."

Thornbury took both her hands in his. "Did I mention how splendid you were, with Mrs Threnod?"

"I can hear it as many times as you care to say it," Mneme replied with a smile. "I *was* magnificent. What has happened with the Countess of Balmady?"

"Still being questioned," he told her. "No one is quite ready to believe she was knowingly in league with an assassin, but they were companions for years. How can she not have known something?"

Mneme had witnessed both women as a tight double act. "I'd keep an eye on her," she agreed. "Her loyalties are compromised, at the very least." Mrs Threnod had given the Countess the sleeping potion — but was that to avert suspicion?

Thornbury squeezed her hands. "I have to go away for a while," he said. "A favour to my father. I'm afraid I don't know when I'll be free."

Mneme could have answered for him: *never*. There would always be another favour, another special request, another mission that only he could handle. She knew that now. "I'm sure I'll find some way to occupy myself," she said with what she hoped was a warm and loving smile.

His face softened. "Miss Seabourne. Mneme. Will you receive me, when I return?"

Inside the covered basket, her new hedgehog sneezed with a sound like the stem of a champagne glass breaking in half. Mneme refused to make any connexion between that, and how her heart felt right now.

"I will always be at home to you, Mr Thornbury," she said quietly. "I look forward to hearing about your adventures. Why, I think you must have the most exciting retirement ahead of you."

He gave her a sheepish smile, and kissed her hand.

The great frost lasted another twenty days. Once it was over, the Frost Fair was remembered as the best that Town had enjoyed in decades. There was, in the end, an elephant, though it turned out to be a rather small one and many children declared it not worth the bother.

The Fenchurches never returned to the ice. In spring, when Mneme delivered a basket of treats for the children to their street address, she learned that some mysterious benefactor had bestowed upon them the funds for a new printing press.

"This model puffs and blows and I don't like it as much as the last one," Mrs Fenchurch grumbled, polishing it with a great deal of pride. "But it's not in the river, and that makes it head and shoulders above the last."

"You're never happy, wife!" teased Mr Fenchurch,

holding the baby while his two sons pawed through the basket Mneme had brought, sorting the sweetmeats into piles.

"Don't you start, or I'll turf you in the river too," Mrs Fenchurch threatened. "Here, Miss Seabourne," she added. "Going to that do at the Continental, are you? We printed all the flyers for that one."

"I am indeed," said Mneme. "I'm looking forward to it."

"Have an ice for me then," said Mrs Fenchurch, grinning widely. "Can't stand the stuff, myself. What's wrong with a good cup of cider to warm the bones?"

THANKS to the recent Frost Fair, the citizens of Town had become quite used to spending time on the river. This inspired some enterprising investor to continue the trend. Within a few weeks of the thaw, the Continental Tearooms had begun rapid construction: a massive floating pavilion that one could only reach by boat, or by portal.

It was the first establishment in the Teacup Isles to openly advertise itself as providing portals for ladies.

Now, a few weeks into spring, they celebrated their grand opening.

"I can't believe we're getting there by swan-shaped boat," complained Lady Liesl, who had optimistically worn a spencer over a day dress instead of heavier layers, and was regretting it. "My bonnet will be all askew by the time we arrive."

"It's the ceremony of the thing," Juno chided, her own velvet pelisse filling rather more of the boat than was altogether fair. "We will purchase our first portal ticket there, to support the charity."

"First ticket," Liesl snorted. "If you knew how much I'd paid in bribes to portal watchmen over the last year…"

"Where will you all go?" Mneme asked, straightening her own bonnet. It was a higher construction of straw and silk than she usually chose, but it had the added benefit of a cozy compartment for her glass hedgehog, Basil, to curl up and nap when he liked. "Through your first official portal, I mean."

"Oh, we're all going to Daisy Afershaw's place," said Juno with a wave of her gloved hand. "You know, the Baron of Dormouse's great-niece? She and her wife have a splendid little seaside apartment three islands from here, where the spring sunshine has actually arrived, and she's filled the bath with champagne. Then everybody back to Storm Bolt for supper, I've ordered a goose and a concert pianist."

"Married lady parties sound so much nicer than catching husband parties," said Liesl wistfully. "I promised my sister I'd bring her an ice from the Continental, all the way to her school on the far side of the Isle of Thyme. It's their open day, so it shouldn't be too difficult. As long as all her little friends don't get wind of it, or I'll be popping back and forth through portals all day, fetching cup after cup of elderflower and pineapple cream."

"But you *can*!" Juno said delightedly. "What a splendid chore. Our Mneme changed the world with her pamphlets, and this will I swear be the last swan-shaped boat I ever set foot in."

The enchanted boat listed slightly, its feathery wings sputtering to a halt. Juno kicked the side and, in a cloud of feathers, they were propelled forward across the river once again.

"I didn't change anything," said Mneme, who had come to terms with this. "The world was ready to change, and I nudged it forward. The Queen did the rest."

"You nudged it in the right direction, which *was* into the lap of the Queen," said Lady Liesl. "That's the trick."

"Take the credit while you can," said Juno. "And we shall all profit from being your friends. The Notorious Miss Mnemosyne Seabourne!" she cheered, and Liesl cheered alongside her.

At the Continental, they were greeted with balloons of brandy, frozen desserts, and a gabble of well-dressed ladies bubbling with excitement. The portals were on display: wide archways draped with ribbons and lace and hot-house flowers because of course, if they were for ladies, they must be ornamental as well as functional.

(Mneme noticed that the width was more generous than with gentlemen's portals, as if the builders anticipated the return of hooped petticoats at some point in the future. If she had to start another campaign to prevent the return of that particular fashion, she would.)

The assembly of ladies was all in a whirl of conversation and sugary treats: everything that Mneme had dreaded about Town before this winter. Mneme was notorious again (still) but her involvement with the Queen's decree in support of portal equality, and the rumours of the Sevinny affair, meant that most of the ladies were far more interested in befriending her than whispering about her behind her back.

This notoriety, at least, was for something she had done and not for the crimes of her family. Mneme still found it exhausting.

When it was her turn to hand over her charity ticket and step through the portal, Mneme did not have to think about her destination. She wrote her address in firm letters and handed it to the attendant.

She was going home.

~

SHELLWICH STANDING, the Seabourne estate, was blissfully quiet for the rest of the spring.

Mneme's mamma, Lady Galatea Seabourne, took to portal travel like a duck to water. Now that the family scandal had died down ever so slightly, she committed herself to visiting everyone she had ever met. She was having so much fun that she hadn't mentioned Mneme's lack of a husband in weeks.

Mneme's papa, much happier now that his wife was not spending all her time huffing and sighing around his favourite haunt on the Isle of Bath, had chosen to stay home and work on a new book about the history of whelks.

Mneme read, and walked, and played with Basil, and sometimes went whole afternoons without speaking a word to anyone. It was blissful.

Yes, she had more visitors than usual, but she had finally convinced Juno and Liesl to at least send a calling card through the portal the night before, so she could be properly braced for their arrival.

She could only hope that, as with portal travel and glass hedgehogs, Mneme's preference for guests to provide notice before visiting would start a fashion.

One morning, she returned from an early walk on the beach to discover a different calling card awaiting her.

"Mr Charles Thornbury is in the sunshine parlour, Miss Seabourne," the housekeeper informed her.

Mneme looked down at her salt-encrusted shoes, her third-best dress, and the hungry glass hedgehog cradled in her arms. "I'll see him right now," she said, and prided herself on not even glancing in a mirror on her way.

She could tell from Mrs Marchwairing's face that she was an utter fright, but if Mr Thornbury didn't want her with windblown hair and sea-damp shoes, then what was the point of him?

He, of course, was very nicely dressed in his usual understated way, with a blue silk cravat he could not have bought for himself (his own preference tended toward the grey, and she knew a Duke and Duchess of Storm gift when she saw one).

As Mneme burst into the room, Mr Thornbury turned to see her, and smiled warmly.

She looked him over, to be certain he was all in one piece.

He did the same to her, then carefully scooped Basil out of her hands and placed him on the sideboard, before kissing her.

Mr Thornbury kissed her, that is, not Basil. Basil was very happy on the sideboard, as he had been eyeing off that poinsettia plant for months.

"Is this all right?" Thornbury asked as they came apart from the kiss.

"Very all right," said Mneme, breathless. "Hello, there. Did you catch your villain?"

"It's more complicated than that."

"It always is. Do you want tea?"

"Certainly."

They made it through three rounds of tea and sandwiches, and all the stories of their time apart, before Mneme finally lost all patience.

"Well? Are you going to ask me to marry you again?"

Thornbury hid a smile. "I rather thought I might. Your father will be terribly disappointed if I don't, as he just spent half an hour explaining whelks to me and he'll have to start over again, if you find a new suitor."

"He does hate meeting new people," Mneme agreed. "Do you have any more secrets I should know about before I say yes? Big ones," she added at the look of alarm on his face. "I understand about state secrets."

Thornbury spread his hands wide. "You are privy to

the worst of my skeletons. In fact, given that you had a recent conversation with my father that neither of you saw fit to inform me about, I would say that you have more than enough reasons to turn me down already."

"Don't get ahead of yourself," said Mneme. "Answer me this: in marrying you, would I be the wife of a spell-cracker, a scholar, a secret agent… or a future spymaster?"

Thornbury blinked, and she saw the realisation cross his face of what it was she had learned from his father. It came as a shock to him, which was more endearing than it should be. "Would that make a difference to your answer?" he managed finally, looking as if he did not know whether to pull out an engagement ring, or jump out the nearest window.

Mneme pushed the tea trolley aside, the better to wind her arms around his neck. "Answer *my* question first, my dear, and we'll find out," she told him.

THE END

GLOSSARY OF THE TEACUP ISLES

SECOND EDITION

- Ambrodes — the most exclusive department store in Town
- Arachne — a famous deviser of criminally excellent spells and hexes using techniques inspired by spider webs and mythical creatures
- Arcade of Ladylike Dainties, the — one of the attractions of Town
- Bath, Isle of — one of the Teacup Isles: a holiday destination with healing waters
- Baths, the — a shared and social space for washing, swimming, and anything else one can think of doing in large, ornate pools of water.
- Bathing machine — a large box structure with a hole in it, used at the seaside to discreetly deposit semi-clad young ladies into the water (and, one would hope, retrieve them afterwards) in a modest fashion
- Blackguard — even more villainous than a cad or a bounder
- Bounder — a cad
- Bumbleton Palace — a palace in the country
- Bundling — a tradition of fitting entire families

   and/or crowds of perfect strangers in the
same bed
- Cad — a bounder
- Cider-wife — a brewer and purveyor of delicious apple- and pear-themed beverages
- Contraception amulets — a most ingenious innovation
- Continent, the — an extremely large island, beyond the Lyric Sea, foreign but fashionable
- Continental Tearooms, the — a floating establishment on the River Scamander, featuring the first public portals specifically provided for the use of ladies
- Croquet, the new — a jolly game involving young ladies, sticks, balls and creative sorcery
- Court of Lords, the — one of the two official government bodies of the Teacup Isles; the aristocratic one
- Dormouse, Isle of — one of the Teacup Isles: a barony and a source of rather good tea
- Fichu — a lace collar, designed to hide one's décolletage and/or keep your neck warm
- Frost Fair — an impromptu gathering of entrepreneurial merchants and entertainers on the surface of a frozen river in a big city, on the rare occasion this is possible; don't even ask about the insurance implications. Sometimes, there's an elephant
- Gaia — a goddess
- Gentlewoman, the — a lady's magazine full of fashion plates, cosmetic recipes and discreet employment advertisements
- Gothic novels — yes, there's always a castle, several secret passages, a governess or other young lady in trouble, and a ghost

- Great Discretion, the — see the Secret Senate
- Hades — the land of the dead
- Ices — a delicious frozen dessert made from flavoured custards and cordials; terribly expensive in summer, and really quite reasonably priced in winter, due to the availability of ice
- Library of Arcane Promises, the — one of the attractions of Town
- Luncheon — a light midday meal often enjoyed by ladies, and occasionally hijacked by gentlemen
- Lyric Sea, the — home to the Teacup Isles
- Magisters — mysterious working magicians, blamed and/or credited for all manner of sinister goings on
- Manticore, Isle of — one of the Teacup Isles: a lordship
- Mantle — a warm and decorative cape, worn around the shoulders of a lady. Also, that shelf over the fireplace.
- Memory, Isle of — one of the Teacup Isles: quiet, peaceful
- Muff — an alternative to or addition to gloves: basically a large cozy pocket, often lined with fur, carried by ladies in order to keep their hands toasty warm in winter. Often worn with tippets — a long, thin scarf arrangements. The subject of many lewd jokes among respectable married people
- Museum of Antiquities, the — one of the attractions of Town
- Muslin — the lightest possible of cotton fabric, very fashionable and worn by ladies in pale

white and cream colours, even when the
weather is far from appropriate
- Muslin Disease, the — catching a cold or lung
  ailment due to insufficient layering of warm
  clothes in winter
- Name day — far more important than
  birthdays, with better presents
- Pantheon Opera House, the — one of the
  attractions of Court
- Parliament of Gentles, the — one of the two
  official government bodies of the Teacup Isles;
  the slightly more egalitarian one
- Pelisse — a winter overgarment worn by ladies,
  somewhere between a tailored coat and a
  ballgown. Layering is important to stay warm!
- Pickled Pear, the — a most excellent cider-
  house with cozy rooms for hire, overlooking the
  River Scamander in Town
- Punch and Judy show — a familiar
  entertainment taking place in a curtained box
  (just large enough for one person inside, very
  portable) featuring puppets who abuse each
  other mightily while making rude jokes and
  playing around with sausages and/or
  truncheons. Certainly not for children
- Ratafia — a fortified wine, flavoured with
  almond, spice or orange blossom; or, in a pinch,
  any fruity punch that is also alcoholic
- Sandwich, Isle of — one of the Teacup Isles:
  an earldom
- Satirical print — a terribly rude cartoon, often
  with political implications
- Secret Senate, the — a completely unofficial
  governing body of the Teacup Isles, made up
  of women. Also known as the Great Discretion

- Scamander — a river of the Isle of Town, dividing it from the central Isle of Court; freezes over every decade or so
- Season — that part of the year when it is warm enough for garden parties, house parties or balls, and unmarried nobility are positively encouraged to court each other in dramatic fashion
- Shellwich Standing — the Seabourne family home, on the isle of Memory
- Spellcracker — a professional person whose specialty is the removal, shielding and dissolving of unwanted magics
- Sprigged muslin — embroidery of little flower details all over, often white on white
- Storm, Isle of — one of the Teacup Isles: a dukedom.
- Storm Bolt — the Duke of Storm's townhouse, featuring four secret passages, twelve maids, three libraries and the best of all possible butlers
- Storm North — the Duke of Storm's country seat
- Swan-shaped boats — the only polite manner of travel between islands for those of the female persuasion.
- Sympathetic magic — a minor form of spellcraft, using objects (often charmed) to form small but significant shifts in reality, will or marital status
- Thyme, Isle of — one of the Teacup Isles: featuring the Agnew estate and the Tower
- Thyme, the Tower of — traditional prison for high-ranking magical criminals and embarrassing relatives

- Troilish Empire, the — a mysterious and distant land which, nevertheless, values croquet
- Town, Isle of — the centre of most social activity in the Teacup Isles, featuring the Isle of Court
- Uranos — a god
- Widow's weeds — black, purple and grey garments, in order to conspicuously present where a widow is in the process of officially mourning her late husband
- Wistworia Palace — a palace in Town

ALSO BY TANSY RAYNER ROBERTS

Thanks so much for reading. Please consider leaving a review.

Sign up for my newsletter, Tea and Links (tinyurl.com/tansyrr), for news, special offers and monthly tea reviews, plus a free story.

Discover how Mneme and Thornbury first met at the Duke of Storm's house party, in the first volume of the Teacup Magic series, **TEA AND SYMPATHETIC MAGIC,** on sale now.

~

I think you'll also enjoy these titles:

UNREAL ALCHEMY (Belladonna U #1)

HOLIDAY BREW (Belladonna U #2)

Light-hearted urban fantasy collections about a geeky student rock band and their friends, attending an Australian university for the magical and unmagical.

~

THE CREATURE COURT

Intrigue, devastating plot twists and sumptuous detail. Immerse yourself in this dark fantasy trilogy inspired by the 1920s.

Cabaret of Monsters (prequel novella)

Book 1. Power & Majesty

Book 2. The Shattered City

Book 3. Reign of Beasts

~

CASTLE CHARMING

It's not easy living in a fairy tale kingdom.

Fall in love with the wild, attention-seeking Princes Charming and the poor suckers who work for them. Spinning wheel curses, giant attack beanstalks, fairy invasions and wishes come true. Plus, kissing. So much kissing!

ABOUT THE AUTHOR

Tansy Rayner Roberts is an award-winning Australian science fiction and fantasy author who never wears corsets or sprigged muslin. She lives with her family in Tasmania and has been known to pick up the occasional embroidery hoop.

Listen to Tansy on Sheep Might Fly, a podcast where she reads aloud her stories as audio serials.

What tea is Tansy drinking? Find out at tinyurl.-com/tansyrr when you subscribe to her excellent newsletter.

Follow TansyRR at:
tansyrr.com/
news@tansyrr.com

* 9 7 8 0 6 4 8 7 6 3 9 9 4 *